Addie Sinclair:
Vortex of
DOOM

ISBN 978-09865001-1-4

PUBLISHER'S NOTE

This is a work of fiction. Names, characters, places and incidents either are the product of the author's overactive imagination or are used fictitiously, and any resemblance to actual persons, living or dead, events or locales is entirely coincidental and all in your head.

Library and Archives Canada Cataloguing in Publication

Clarke, Kimberley

Addie Sinclair: Vortex of Doom / Kimberley Clarke

I. Title Pink Wig Publishing

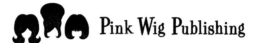 Pink Wig Publishing

West Vancouver, British Columbia V7S 3G4

Printed in Canada

— For Donald, Maddison, Kelsey and Jet. —

Acknowledgements

Serious gratitude and thanks go out to Leanne Prain for her editing genius and turn of phrase, Diane Farnsworth for being an ink sistah and cheerleader, and JFly, again, for his graphic magic

Addie Sinclair: Vortex of DOOM

Kimberley Clarke

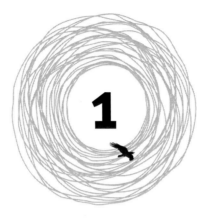

"Wakey, wakey rise and shine kiddo! The early bird gets the worm, ya know. Saturday morning is retail's Holy Grail and the bus is leaving in fifteen minutes.** Shake a leg, Addie. Wake up, make, then smell the coffee. HAH! Up and at 'em." My dad cackles at me through my door.

This is the list of Saturday morning clichés that I hear from my Dad every weekend.

This is the list of Saturday morning clichés that I recite in my sleep.

This is the list of Saturday morning clichés that I always ignore. I wish his glad tidings had a snooze button that I could push. He is such a kidder – a giant annoying alarm clock of a kidder.

I don't want to get up. Instead I'll roll over and nest under the blankets. I feel the cool October breeze that's sneaking through my window. I'll just breathe in some fresh fall air and enjoy the comfort and sanity of my room.

"Ah—deeee. Ah—dee. Are you awake dear? Can you help me for a moment please? Ah—dee?"

The trilling sound of my mom's voice saves me from a dream about drowning. Lately, I have been having a lot of these. Ms. Plunkett, the school counsellor that works with me and my mom and dad, calls them 'stress dreams'. They occur when you feel overwhelmed by stuff and they are so creepy. In the last two weeks, there have been a few times when I have woken up gasping for air. So I am glad to hear my mom's voice. I am awake and alive.

"Addie, for heaven's sake, it's almost two o'clock. I can't wait forever. Get up please."

"Okay, okay." I grumble, "Hold yer freakin' horses."

Even though I sound crabby I am secretly glad to be awake. I scuffle down the stairs into the kitchen in my giant fuzzy pink bunny footie pj's and aim directly for the coffee maker. The kitchen is clean; my favourite Peter Rabbit mug is sitting by the coffee pot; and I can hear my mother making sounds of industry in the garage. It's great to know that I am getting up late in a relative calm, and not because I am avoiding my catatonic mother. Aside from the odd stress dream, I have been able to sleep comfortably these past few weeks. Mom is organizing her Halloween decorations while trying to stay out of trouble. Sun streams through the windows, and the warmth mingles with the scent of another one of my mom's brand new hobbies, baking. To distract herself from pain she keeps busy by making delicious treats. Not only does baking help Mom behave, but dad and I benefit from her new talent as there are always cookies and cakes in the house.

Now Cliffie, aka my Dad, has yet another reason to call my mom "Deelicious Dee".

Egad!

My mom has been trying hard, to be well – behaved and sober. Actually, we all have. I see Ms. Plunkett and Dr. Rubin, the psychologist who helps run group, at least once a week. Mom and Dad have seen both of them a couple of times but we know that things won't change much until Mom's pain is under control. Mom's doctor, Dr. Gilbert, is working on that. If he is not able to balance things out, it's off to rehab for mom. Dad is not too thrilled with the possibility of losing his delicious Dee. I am an impossibly awful cook. Being stuck alone with me for an unknown number of weeks will mean eating canned spaghetti, which is definitely not delicious.

"Addie, can you please come here a minute? I have a box of stuff I would like you to put on the kitchen table. And I found a stretched canvas. Do you think Sigge might want it?" She calls through the inside doorway to the garage.

"Oh probably, yer mom-ness. I'll be right there."

I saunter over to the door and almost fall over as I look over my mom's shoulder.

"Oh Mom! You haven't done this in years! It's completely amazing. It's the best one ever. You must be feeling better! Can I give you a hug please?"

The garage has been transformed into the most incredible creepy haunted house extravaganza; cobwebs, green and purple sparkly skeletons, fake dismembered bodies, cauldrons and rats. It is filled with all of the things little kids love to see on

Halloween. Mom used to decorate like this every year when I was little and it was always so spooky and magical. Having a mom that was creative and artistic always made me feel special, even though sometimes it meant that she acted a little loopy. Her pumpkin carvings would have put Martha Stewart to shame. Actually, Martha Stewart probably got all her ideas from my mom. Mom is that good.

"Thank-you sweet-pea. I thought I should do something for the neighbourhood this year, you know? Maybe as a kind of peace offering? What do you think? Do you think anyone will come or let their kids in our yard?"

Mom winces at this realization.

"Are you kidding me, Mom? The minute you open the garage door you will have all the neighbourhood kids begging to come through here! It's beautiful, in its own very creepy way and if you have a giant bowl of treats, the attendance will be bigger than dad's ego!"

I smile at my mom. I forget how sweet she truly is.

But I can't forget that addiction is a very nasty thing. It separates you from what you know and love. It's a slope and it's a really slippery long way down.

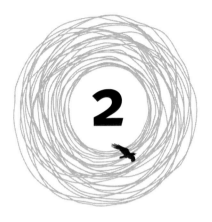

2

I have it somewhere. I know I do. I've got to. I don't lose important stuff.

This place **stinks**. It is a complete, freakin' dump and it stinks.

No wonder I can't find anything. **I can't think 'cause it stinks.**

I have got to get organized. Got to finally take out the garbage.

As soon as I do, I know I will find what I need. Really, and when I do, **they will know they have been found.** They've got stuff I can use, stuff they will come to share.

But right now, this second, I need a chocolate bar, a coffee, and a little sumpthin' you know, to pick me up. Where's my other sneaker? Fffft who cares. I'm wearin' a sock.

See ya later you complete effin' stinkin' dump.

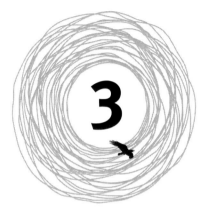

3

The coffee has finished brewing. I get out some cookies, ginger snaps to be exact, and the sugar and cream for mom and me. There is absolutely nothing like the first coffee of the morning, from your very own coffee maker, even if that morning happens to be 2pm after sleeping in on a Saturday. Coffee's a warm and cuddly way to start the day; slowly and with sweet and rich cookies to savour the sight of the sun and October blue skies.

I love this time of year. Endings lead to new beginnings. Snow is not far off. Any time after the thirty-first of October is almost a snow day. You can smell the frost and the clean-ness of the first snow air. The dust dies and the air clears its throat. But so far this year, there has been no frost, or cold weather, only the dog days of Indian summer. I am not complaining though. I think I am a California girl at heart. I love the sun and the heat. But really, I must tell you that I would like an Ice Age to have frozen over the last few months, leaving them to fossilize and turn into precious artifacts for some future explorer. I certainly don't need to relive them any time soon.

The box I carried in from the garage is in the middle of the table. I lift the lid to take a peek at its contents. Inside I see a cherry red wig and some aquamarine coloured sequins. But, and this is a giant but, before I get to savour the contents and roll around in some nostalgia, someone pounds at the door. Sigge's outline appears through the gauzy orange lace curtain. I can tell she is anxious because she is swaying back and forth from one foot to the other. She is even flipping her hair.

I take my time answering the door. Well not really, what's the diff between five and seven seconds? Rather than jump, I step. I slowly unlock the door and open it about forehead width.

"Yesssss. Can I help you?"

I can see from the look on her face that Sigge has some news, and it's big, and she is in no mood for teasing. She muscles her way past me and goes into the kitchen. It is if the cookie jar has magnetic powers and Sigge is drawn towards it.

"Sigge take a look at what my…"

She cuts me off mid-sentence.

"Addie, did you hear the news on the radio? There is a posse of coyotes terrorizing a cemetery. We have to plan an excursion."

Sigge plants herself by the kitchen table, one hand is on her hip the other firmly grips her phone which is encrusted with purple crystals.

She must have found her Bejeweller and did I just catch a whiff of lavender?

"You are kidding, right? A cemetery and a pack of wild coyotes. These two things together sound like a good idea to you?" I shake my head and sigh at her.

"Oh, it only gets better. You know which cemetery it is? It's the one out on Highway 13. The historical one on the way to the Old Fort. Oh-mi-gawd, Addie we can find out if the rumour is true, just like we always wanted. These coyotes have done us a huge favour!"

As Sigge rambles, she holds her phone and rummages through the treat jar. She finds the Dino Fruit Chewies, and looks back at me. I can see that she is serious. Her steel grey eyes are the size of cookies.

I must be hungry.

"Really Addie. Actually. They are terrorizing the cemetery. The pack has actually stopped people from placing flowers on plots. Can you believe this? I love this story. I need to know if it's true." Sigge pops blue and orange dinosaurs into her mouth between sentences.

"Are you having some sort of weird Twilight moment, Sig? You want to go and find out if coyotes hunt in packs in cemeteries? Consult with your local television listings for the nature channel my friend. It's warmer, less weird, and much safer don't cha know. And how are we going to get there, by the way? Did you ever think of that?" I ask.

"Wolves, Addie. Wolves. Good Grief. Get your literary allusions straight okay? Twilight was wolves and vampires. Follow me now, w-o-l-v-e-s and v-a-m-p-i-r-e-s. There was nary, and I mean nary, a mention of coyotes in that series. And anyway the coyotes are not really what I am interested in, so the nature channel won't help. As you can see I have thought this through and I can anticipate your arguments. Honours English and the debate club do pay off. I anticipate and refute. Cool huh!" Sigge smiles and squishes a red chewy dino through the gap in her front teeth. "Oh and Bernerd will take us."

"How are we three going to get there on his scooter? Are you and I going to both put on the same coat, same shirt, same pants, same gloves, and be the two- headed freak on the back of the Vespa pretending that we are one person?"

"I can't believe I never thought of that Addie, that is so cool. Let's try it!" she says with more enthusiasm than I can believe.

"Are you kidding me Sigge? For serious? I was being sarcastic."

"Yes my friend I am. Both kidding about the Vespa and serious about the cemetery. Get rid of those fuzzy bunny footie-jammies and let's get planning."

"Okay, when did you want to go?" I am resigned to the fact that Sigge's enthusiasm is really hard to turn down but it's also Saturday and my fuzzy bunny footie-jammies must stay.

"Well, let's consult the calendar for an appropriate "rendez-vous with the apparitions" date. We need to go to the cemetery on the night of the full moon to see if the ole' ghost story is true. Mwa-haha."

"I don't know about this Sig. What if the legend is true? What if a car mysteriously materializes out of thin air and that there really is a guy dressed all in black and woman dressed all in white who drift around? What if? I don't know Sig, it sounds kinda fun but it also sounds, well, like I may possibly have a horrible and embarrassing digestive tract accident." I stammer.

"Are you kidding me? You can be such a jam-tart sometimes, Addie. If you are so scared Bernerd and I will go by ourselves. You can stay home and knit."

Sigge is really ticked at me. I know this because she loves to knit and normally she would never "dis" the knittin'. She is also shaking my dad's disco ball calendar at me. Why would anyone make a calendar out of disco ball photographs? And why would my dad own one? It takes him back to kinder, gentler, dancey times I guess.

"Okay, okay. I give up. Let's set a date. When is the full moon? What date is it today?" I ask.

"Today is October sixteenth. So if this calendar is correct the full moon occurs at exactly this time in a week. This is perfect, Addie. Next Saturday, the twenty-third at 1:36 a.m. is the totally, completely full-freaky moon. We have seven days to get physically and mentally prepared. I will do a little research to see if there is some kind of coyote repellent. You can find out if there is something we can bring to keep us safe while enticing spirits to visit us. Is this not the most excellent of plans, Add? I am so excited I could just ooze ectoplasm."

Sigge is dancing around the kitchen like a wild thing. Maybe I should restrict her chewy dino treat intake. She seems to over-react to sugar.

"Alright. Now that this is settled let's get down to some serious research. I am going to go home and look-up whatever I can about the hauntings and the ghost stories. I'll call you later.

I can't believe we are finally going to do this. Ohmigawd. This is completely aweso....." Sigge's conversation with herself trails off when door closes behind her.

I twirl my way back to the contents of the mystery box.

"Ahhhhh. Oh mom! You found my Ariel costume. This is my favourite costume of all time. Ohmigawd. Check this out," I say as I pull the wig onto my head, "How do I look? Could I get away with dying my hair this color? What do you think? Do you love it? I love it, I really truly love it." I am posing and sucking in my cheeks to look modelesque..

Mom emerges from the hall and smiles when she sees me. She's all toothy and eye squinty. Sweet and sincere.

"Oh Addie. It looks so cute on you. I can't believe time has gone so fast. One minute you are a little mermaid and the next you're, you're…"

I stop looking at my reflection in the side of the toaster to watch a single tear run down my mom's cheek. It falls down the length of her arm to her elbow to the back of her hand, landing on the kitchen tabletop.

"A really big mermaid? This costume fits my leg. Don't be sad mom. It is a very sweet memory. What else is in there?" I like to distract her from sadness, she can be like a little kid at the grocery store check-out clamouring for gum.

"Oh my. Do you remember these costumes Addie? They were from that fun party at Dot and Bob's place. Remember? Daddy went dressed as a giant baby and I was his hillbilly babysitter? Here is the diaper and my yellow braids and the googly glasses. What a wonderful night that was. You pack of kids went trick or treating and then returned to a wonderful party that had witch finger cookies and ice formed to look like eyeballs. Dot and I had such fun making and planning all of that. Your dad and Bob set off fireworks and set the field out back on fire. The fire department came and, wow, that feels like such a long time ago too!"

The memory makes mom look wistful.

I wonder if I am the only member of my family that realizes that all of our memories have disasters attached to them.

"What are you going to do with all of that stuff, Mom?" I ask. "You can't have the wig. It still fits me and who knows when I'll need a disguise?"

"One of the ladies at the Women's Committee from the Ballet asked me if we had any old costumes, so I dug around and here they are. I wanted to get them cleaned up and organized before Tuesday."

"Cool. Seeing as how we are sorta on the topic, um, Mom, have you ever been to the church out on Highway 13?"

"Well, yes I have Addie, and so have you. Remember? It was the day you got sunstroke. It was about five summers ago when Auntie Laura came to visit. We went there and we went to the Old Fort. I remember you became quite fascinated with one of the headstones. It was a marker for a three year old child. The headstone was incredibly beautiful and had a very intricate carving of a wild rose vine. When we were leaving to go to the fort, I remember your dad said "People are just dying to come here!" and Auntie Laura couldn't stop laughing. We were making fun of the place, but I remember that you treated that place with respect.

No wonder I don't remember. I was overheated and itchy.

"Is it haunted?" I ask, absently scratching my arm.

"I don't know Addie. There are always ghost stories and folk-tales about cemeteries. Why are you asking?"

"What kind of spooky stories are there about that church? Do you know any? Can you tell me? I am doing a little research for, um, school." I pull my chair closer to the table, pick up my coffee mug and settle in to listen really closely.

"I do." Mom clears her throat and in a conspiratorial voice she says, "According to local legend, if you go to the cemetery by the church on the night of the full moon, and if you run around the church counter clock-wise three times you will disappear. Poof. Gone. Into thin air." With that, my mom sits back in her chair and takes a big sip of her coffee. "I haven't thought of that story in years. Goodness Addie. I guess dredging up those costumes and making the haunted garage have got me in a spooky ghost story kind of mood."

At the word "poof" every hair on my body stands at attention. I have never heard this story before. It's creepy yet cool at the same time. I should call Sigge and let her in on this. She'll love this story. I am about to reach for our decrepit rotary dial land line, but I am interrupted by the familiar sound of wind chimes.

"Did you hear that Addie? It sounded like bells or something. How strange. Just as I was talking about spooky ghost stories. Creepy." My mom shakes off the weirdness. "Well I better not lollygag any longer if I want to finish up decorating the garage. I'll be out there if you need me."

I hear it again, muffled, as if it is far off in the distance, as if from *another dimension*!

Wait a minute. The sound is coming from the direction of the treat jar. Sigge's phone is in the treat jar. I rummage around and dig it out. I bet it's Sigge calling, looking for her phone. I better answer it.

"Hey your phone was in the treat jar. That's what took me so long to answer it. Hello? Sigge? Is that you? Your phone is here at my house. In my kitchen. Hello?"

"Uh hi. Is this Sigge?" a somewhat familiar male voice asks. I feel an odd slight breeze brush my cheek.

"No. I asked you the same thing. Who is this? Bernerd are you drunk? If you are I am going to be so annoyed with you. After all we have been through the last few weeks? You have some nerve."

"Who is this if this is not Sigge? Why do you have her phone?"

"This is Addie. She left it here a couple of…. And why do you care? Who is this?"

"This is Er –er Kevin. Her cousin. Kevin Baxter. Addie I must say, you have a really great phone voice. Really cute. Kinda sexy. I bet you look as good as you sound."

At that last comment my hairs are, again, standing at attention. This is such a weird conversation. I must be wound up because of my mom, her ghost story and an errant wisp of wind.

"I dunno. Maybe. Kevin Baxter huh? Why don't you call Sigge on her home phone? You'll be able to reach her there, for sure." I offer.

"Actually I can't. My mom, Sigge's um, aunt you know, is planning, um, a surprise birthday party for, um, Sigge's dad, and they are so good at figuring out plans and such that I figure that the less time actually talking to someone in that house the less time it will take them to figure out all the plans and stuff. You know how these things go. Being sneaky is a good quality when you are planning a party."

"Right. Gotcha. I planned a surprise party once that wasn't. Bummer. Not for the guest of honour but for me. I was busted within fifteen minutes of the idea. I don't lie well."

"Okay Addie. Is that short for something like oh, say, beautiful?"

"That was really cheesy. Is there something I can do for you Kevin Baxter? If not I have to go and return this phone to Sigge."

"There is actually. Want to have coffee? Tonight maybe? Sixish? Help me plan the party. There are two conditions, though."

"Okay. What are they?"

"One, um, you have to pick the place for coffee, and two you can't tell Sigge or Bernerd about this call. I mean it. If they are aware that I am trying to track them down, they will know something is up and the surprise will be blown."

"Okay. I guess Brewster's is the place and I do understand about not saying anything. But I can't make it tonight. It'll have to be Monday. They are pretty perceptive. I'll see you sixish at Brewster's, Monday. Bye. Don't forget."

"What? Really? Monday? For Ffffu… um heaven's sakes. Why so long? That feels like forever Abbie to um, meet you …. Bye Abbelicious," says Kevin, his voice suddenly chocolate thick and much too honey sweet.

"Howdy, unknown caller," giggles Sigge.

"Sigge. We are in luck. "My mom knows some of the folklore about the church. And, I found your phone."

"No way, really Add? Where was the rascal? And what did your Mom say about the church? Spare me no details."

Sigge is one of the most curious people I know. It figures that Kevin wouldn't want her to know about our conversation. She is very intuitive, or as she likes to say an "outstanding investigative individual".

"Well, as my mom was cleaning out the garage to construct an especially spooky haunted house she found a bunch of our family's old costumes. She told me, that, if, on the night of the full moon, you run counter clock-wise around the church, you will disappear. Isn't that wild? Oh and your phone was in the treat jar and my mom has a blank canvas for you. It's huge."

"Actually? My phone was in the treat jar? How did you find it? Did you run around the jar three times? Hah."

Hmmmm. This is a little awkward. How am I not going to reveal the secret?

"What's the name of your bank?" I ask, stalling for an idea.

"What? That's random. I go to the credit union. You know the one with the cool hair commercials on TV? That one. Trudy, my hair stylist did the hair for the commercial. Why?"

"Oh, uh– they phoned. I saw their name on your call display.

Lucky for you ! Your phone may have been lost for days."

"Nah. Not a chance. Now that I know your treat jar is filled with the gelatine of the gods, I will be there anon or sooner. Thank your mom for the potential huge painting."

"Okay," I answer. See you soonish I guess."

Phew. I hope her intuition was less than finely tuned today and that little lie went undetected.

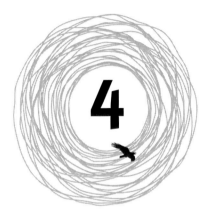

For the last couple of hours all I have been able to think about is asking Sigg if she would ever go on a blind party planning date with a guy that she has only talked to once on the phone. But I can't ask her. Instead I spend the rest of the afternoon making Halloween crafts with my mom. Keeping Mom busy makes the both of us occupied with healthy and happy thinking and it keeps her creative juices juicy. Additionally, I get the benefit of a really cool haunted garage that will be the envy of every serious halloweener in a ten mile radius. I also don't have to lie to Sigge's face about my "other" adventure. So, after dinner when Sigge came to pick up her phone and just as I was telling her about the pair of red floating eyes and the lavender scented wind that follow only some people in the cemetery, my bedroom door almost fell off its hinges and we both said together,

"Holy crap!"

"What was that?" Sigge managed to choke out in the

immediate after silence of the visitation.

"Shhhhh. It'll hear us." I whisper.

"Ohmigawdohmigawd!" quivered Sig.

Another whomp but not as insistent this time and with a disembodied voice attached to it.

"Addie. Could you open your door dear? Sigge are you in there?"

"Yes I am." She croaks.

"Could either of you pull yourself away from your fear and open the door please? It's only me."

"It's only my mom. Could you let me go? Sigge – unclench me please. How are we actually going to sit in a cemetery and wait for the unknown if we are scared in my safe, warm and obviously un-ghosty room?" I hiss and lunge for the door.

There is a huge canvas with feet and fingers and hair on the other side of the door. Mom Bob Squarepants.

"Heavens girls. What could you possibly have been talking about that would shake you up so? Sigge please stop shaking. I found this canvas in the garage. Would you like it? I have no intention of painting any time soon so why don't you steady yourself and take it out of my hands."

"Are you kidding me Mrs. S.? That is so great! I would love it. I have an idea already. Here let me get that. Addie. I am going to take this home right now. This is so exciting. I was hoping to save up for a canvas and now here it is. Oh man creative visualization is an amazing life tool. This is great. Thank-you so much. Are you sure you don't want it, Mrs. Sinclair?"

Sigge is staggering down the stairs with the canvas, into the kitchen, toward the door. "I will see you at school on Monday, Ad. Tonight and tomorrow I will now be arteesting. Oh and also going for dinner at my Nana's. Addie close the door behind me would you please? Mrs. Sinclair this potential painting is going to be dedicated to you. See you soon. Thanks again."

She made a really fast exit which under the circumstances was understandable and completely perfect. You should never let anyone stand in the way of artistic or divine inspiration I always say. Or do today anyway. Especially since keeping anything from Sigge is virtually impossible when she is in my face.

So determining what to wear on my "date" is a challenge without my wing-person. I want to look trustworthy yet party appropriate. I am so glad Kevin agreed on Monday to meet because Sigge has piano lessons on Mondays and therefore is always anxious to get home from school. This means that I won't have to come up with a story about why I can't walk home with her. This feeling is so sucky. This is why I don't keep secrets very well. I get nervous and trip myself up. So I want to be casual, but not so casual that Kevin will think I am just home from PE and I am sweaty and gross. Comfortable so that I am not constantly adjusting or scratching but not fleece, never polar fleece. There is something about clothing that is made out of recycled pop bottles that seems wrong, not only for this meeting but completely in general. AND I will have to survive the whole day at school besides, fielding clothing questions.

"So Addie. Do you have a job interview? A meeting with your parole officer? Hot Yoga? Are you a sandwich artist?" My closet is not big enough for all these questions and the prospect of

Monday feels overwhelming already. Thank goodness I have Sunday to plan.

"Maaaaaaaawm. Can you come here a minute? I reallllllllllly neeeeeed to talk to you." I howl like death is my new best friend.

"Goodness Adelaide. What is it? Are you all right? Did you get your leg caught in some sort of trap? That was a very good, appropriate but serious howl for so early on a Monday." Mom says as she peeks into my room as she opens the door.

"Oh mom. I feel so crappy. My stomach hurts, my wisdom teeth are trying to crack wise and my head feels like it is the size of a very healthy pumpkin. I don't think it's a good idea that I go to school today. A good snooze will fix me right up. Did I mention every joint in my body is aching and I seem to have flu-like symptoms?"

"Addie if you don't feel well enough to go to school get back into your jammies, get yourself a cup of warm milk and crawl right back into bed. You won't learn anything if you are distracted. If it is a virus or something you really do not want to infect your classmates. They wouldn't like that kind of sharing. I will be here for a while dear, but I have a doctor's appointment this afternoon. I will check in on you before I leave. Goodness Addie. I hope you haven't contracted something really serious."

"I will be fine Mom. A little rest is exactly what I need. Good luck with your appointment. Don't forget to tell him about your latest garage creation and take the doctor some of those witch

finger cookies. Oh man, forget the warm milk. I need some sleep."
I assume the wilted violet position. I fall back onto my pile of
shaggy lime-green pillows while the back of my right hand drapes
elegantly yet obviously very weak and ill across my fevered brow.
My mom takes leave of my sanctuary.

*Did she roll her eyes as she left my room? Impossible. My
performance was perfectly pitched.*

Perfect. I will be left alone and to my own devices. I will plan
the perfect party, the perfect coffee date ensemble, and a very perfect witchy weekend midnight picnic all from the comfort of the
"Addie-zone". Perfectly mwaw- haha perfect.

5

I arrive at Brewster's Coffee Coop at exactly 5:30. It is the most comforting smell I know. I inhale the air as deeply as I can; chocolate and cinnamon smell so delicious together.** I do not want to be late for my meeting with Kevin and I want to get the perfect table so that I can watch the door. I place my order, a half-sweet peppermint mocha, and keep my eye on my table. My feet are ready to spring into action if it looks as if someone is going to grab it from under my nose. My favourite table and everyone else's too, has two big red leather chairs on either side of a round mosaic coffee table. The mosaic is made of star-shaped blue and yellow tiles on a red background. It is cheerful and bright and positive; perfect for party planning. Maybe I should suggest a primary color scheme for the party. Who doesn't like primary colors? Is Sigge's dad turning 40 or 50? That would definitely determine my suggestions. I hope Kevin has some good ideas too. This could be really fun. If I get stumped I could ask my mom. My mom, what a perfect resource.

"Half-sweet peppermint mocha for here on the bar!"

Bryson, my favourite barista, shrieks from behind the espresso machine. He's my favourite because he listens to what you ask for and he looks you in the eye when you are placing your order. He takes his job very seriously and his drinks are delicious. Not to mention that he is really good looking and you kinda feel like he has conferred a blessing on you and your drink. A water into mocha kinda moment.

"Thanks Bryson. This looks delicious as only you can make them!" I flirt and move toward the red chairs. I pick the one closest to the door.

"That's my job. Enjoy." Curt and to the point. Emotionless. Company man. Polite to a fault and unaware of his effect on the high school females of Silverwoods.

I place my coffee mug on the table and sit down. I can't decide how to sit. Should I cross my legs, at the knee or the ankle, or should I swing my legs over the rolled arm and look as casual as I do at home. I grow more fidgety and nervous the closer it gets to six o'clock. I have worn my favourite jeans and red converse sneakers, a turquoise hoodie and a yellow tank top. I look bright and cheerful and totally festive. I look, if I must say so myself, approachable and friendly. *I hope he likes me. I hope he thinks I am cute or gorgeous or what am I doing? This meeting is about a party for his uncle first, and then me, maybe, well, second.*

As I am having this ridiculous conversation in my head a tall, let's say six foot two inch blonde really skinny guy enters Brewsters. I don't notice him until he clears his throat. He looks lost and confused and out of his element. So much for positioning myself facing the door so I won't be taken by surprise. I stand up and wave him over to the table.

"Hey. Hi. Are you Kevin? He nods a very tentative nod and smiles a half smile.

"Hi. Um, it's me, Addie. I extend my hand to shake his. He looks at my hand as if it is a dead fish. I wipe my nervousness off on my thigh. 'Have a seat. What kind of drink can I get you?" I ask.

"Oh yeah. Hi." He says rather sheepishly and quietly. His voice doesn't sound anything like it did on the phone the other day. That Kevin was cocky and confident. This Kevin keeps looking over his shoulder.

"Do you mind if we change tables? Let's take that one in the very back, away from the windows. I can't take a chance on being seen." Kevin says.

"No I guess not." I say "I understand how you don't want to spoil the surprise so soon in the planning process. Can't take a chance on blowing your cover."

"Would you like a drink?" I ask again a little more loudly.

"What? A drink? Oh no." Kevin responds as if asking him if he would like a drink is the weirdest thing to ask. He seems really distracted.

"So um, Kevin. About the party. How old is Sigge's dad anyway? Did you have any ideas about where you want to have the shindig or what kind of color scheme? What exactly did your mom have in mind for the surprise? Did she give you any ideas about what she is planning? Before I can help out I need to know some basic info. Like when exactly is she planning on having the surprise?" I cock my head to the right, attempting to look both attentive and cute and focussed.

Kevin stares at me. I stare at him. I look into his very dark smoke grey eyes. They are not deep or pool like. They are flat and unresponsive. He is obviously from some distant side of the Baxter clan. The Baxters I know have eyes that give fireworks competition.

"Uh Kevin? Hello? Can you give me a hint?" This guy is really un-Baxterlike.

"Oh. Oh yeah. Actually, let's get out of here. Let's go find out where they live, I mean let's walk by their house. My, um, mom wants to see if there is a lane where she can get into the house undetected or if there is somewhere she can park a bunch of cars and not be suspicious, you know."

"But I am not finished my drink yet. Don't you want to have something? Water? Anything?" I sound like I am pleading.

"Look. What's with you? I said I didn't want a drink. I still don't want a drink. How about you give me the five bucks the drink would cost you and you can forget about it? Will that make you happy? Hmmm? Let's go." Kevin spits his voice at me through clenched teeth and looks at me with eyes that Edgar Allen Poe would have feared.

"Calm down Kev. It's a coffee. Good grief."

I notice Bryson noticing me or actually Kevin. *I hope Bryson's jealous.*

"Excuse me, Miss Adelaide, you forgot your change," Bryson says very deliberately. "Can you come and get it please? I don't want you to forget it, again."

"Sorry Kevin. In all the excitement of the anticipated party planning I apparently have lost my mind and some change. I will be right back. We'll go in a sec." I chirp.

Kevin shrugs and his neck disappears into his hoodie. His ears appear to be resting on his shoulders. He suddenly looks very small.

"Are you okay?" asks Bryson under his breath as he leans over the counter and whispers into my earring.

I nod.

"Are you sure?" he says staring deeply into my eyes as if I am giving him a drink order.

"Yes I am sure. Really. Why?" I ask as Bryson stares at the inert Kevin over my shoulder.

"I don't know, but if you need anything I am right here. Holler. Whistle. Whatever."

"O–kay. Whistle? Actually?"

"Yeah. Whistle. Oh never mind."

Geez was I ever wrong. Bryson is a bit of a nut.

"Kev, I can call you Kev can't I? Let's get out of here." I turn around from my conversation with Bryson and roll my eyes at Kevin. "You can walk me home."

"So do you live anywhere near Sigge?" Kevin asks.

"Yup. Sure do. Just down the street."

"Could you point their house out to me on the way past?"

He looks like he is trying to smile but it hurts.

"I thought you were their cousin. How could you not know where they live?"

"I haven't been to their new house since they moved in. They always um, visit us at our house, you know. That's why my mom wants me to scout out the 'hood."

"Oh yea. That makes sense. They moved into their place last March before the end of the last school year. What grade are you in or are you finished school?" Small talk will get me home soon.

"I am finished high school. I am in my second year at college, kinda."

"That's cool," I say. "What are you studying?"

"Stuff. So where is their house?"

He is really evasive.

"It's the blue one on your right, right there. See. It has the palm tree in the front yard. We don't have many back lanes here. Cul de sac neighbourhoods don't. They are all a series of circles. Perfect little worlds. Your mom might have to park in the cul de sac behind ours if she wants to really surprise her brother."

"My mom? What? Oh yeah, yeah. Parking. Ya know Abbie, you have been really helpful. See ya. I have really, really gotta go."

"It's Addie. Addie. So will you call me and we can plan some more…" I say to his retreating back.

And with that Kevin runs full speed into the dark while shaking his head and saying "Noooooope".

We didn't make any plans at all.

Palm trees, blue house, palm trees blue house,

palmtreesbluehousebombbreeze,two houses blue trees palm houses

that's some

crazy shi.......

6

It was hard getting up this morning. I had that sleep of navy blue, weird and shadowy dreams. Kevin was in them. He was swimming in freezing cold and dirty murky water. When I finally did get to sleep, it was time to get up. You know how that goes. Anyhow, I didn't shower, swung the hair into a knot, and here I am. Not that I remember actually walking to school but the path is beaten into the sidewalk. I can't get too lost. This is such a strange time of day. It feels apocalyptic. I am alone when there should be kids everywhere. I am only a little late but the streets are deserted and quiet. Everyone is in their place except me. The dream is still with me. I can't seem to shake its ennui.

I follow my feet through the doors of the school closest to my Geography class. Lockers line the halls. I see kids attempting to force the lockers closed, stuffing their day into the small cubicles. I look to my left and see a couple of my seventh favourite friends leaning, as cool and removed as they can, up against the lockers.

There is Lola, Goth du jour, with her ten feet of black eyeliner and her bestie, Stacey. No wait, that's not Stacey that's OMIGAWD. I can't believe this. I actually scurry into class, mouse-like and furtive, to my desk.

Sigge is in her desk and her face lights up as she sees me.

"Is everything okay? What's with your posture? I was worried 'cause you weren't at the corner this morning."

"Yeah, sorta. Everything's kinda fine. Weird dreams and wacky visions have spun me off my axis this morning. Not to mention the wild scene outside the classroom." I say eyes bugging and my head pointing toward the door.

Lola and Lindsay saunter into the room, both snug in variations of black leather.

Lindsay Dixon, my former best friend of all time. Pleather.

Lola Lambert. Real-deal.leather

Lindsay. Seems. To. Have. A. New. Best. Friend.

Lola takes her usual seat behind me and Lindsay sits in the back left corner. Lindsay is looking different, cooler and paler somehow, and I wonder how it happened. Lola is like she always is; separate and apart, yet connected and cool. All worlds in the palm of her hand. It doesn't hurt that she's freakin' uber smart, she finished twelfth grade history in grade six and tutored the seniors that same year, and has a rock star for a dad. He's the lead singer for Dim Dark and the Persuaders. I like and I fear Lola. Much like the current relationship with myself.

"Whoa-o-o! Isn't that an interesting combo-o!" shivers Sigge as they walk past and churn up a frosty breeze in their wake.

"Scary combo, if you ask me." I whisper. "Super-sized NASTY."

God forbid Lola hears me. She has a wicked tongue and a brain to match. You want to stay on her good side. Rumour has it she may be a real magic practicing witch.

"Sigge have you checked the long range forecast? Do you have any idea what the weather is going to be like on Friday?" I am inspired to ask a weather related question as we are starting our new unit on climatology in Geo. Sigge turns around decisively in her desk and looks me straight in the eyes.

"As a matter of fact I have Ad. Clear as a bell, with only a slight chance of frost. Perfect midnight picnic weather. I am so psyched you have no idea. Bern has picked up..."

Before Sigge could finish her thought she is interrupted by Ms. Clayton.

"Ladies. If your conversation is weather related I am sure we would all like to hear about it. Turn around Sigge, please." Sigge does as she is told and I attempt to bail us out.

"Actually, Ms. Clayton we were discussing the possibility of having a meteorologist come and talk to us about weather. You know the guy, Mr. Rod Rivers, the cute guy who delivers the weather on SKYWATCH TV? He offers classrooms the opportunity of having him come in and talk about how to predict the weather. And Sigge here has done some preliminary research and has determined that this Friday will be clear but, like this very moment, a little frosty." I say this and hear a couple of sniggers from the desk behind me.

"Nice one Sinclair." Lola snorts. "Excellent save."

Ms. Clayton stares into the back right corner of the classroom with a rather bemused look on her cherry red lipsticked lips.

"What an excellent idea, Addie. See what you can organize for us."

"I would love to Ms. Clayton. Maybe I can even score you a date…"

Ms. Clayton is one of those teachers that you can tease and she won't think that you are being an insubordinate snot.

"Well we'll see 'bout that won't we!" she says as she launches into a lesson on thermoclines. I probably made her day.

"Sinclair. Pssst. I can help you," whispers Lola. "Trust me. Tell her you can have him here for next class. Really."

"What? I wasn't serious Lola."

"Just work with me here. Tell her, Addie." Lola pokes me in the back with her pen for punctuation.

I stick up my hand and start waving it around like a lunatic. Sigge is shaking her head.

"Yes Addie. You can go to the washroom." Ms. Clayton says automatically.

"No uh I don't need to go. I just wanted to let you know that um, according to a text that I just received, I know, I shouldn't be receiving texts in class, but in the service of securing us a meteorologist, Mr. Rod Rivers will be joining us for next class. For true and everything. So just sayin'. Meteorologist on deck! Whoot!"

I can't believe I am going to trust Lola. Good grief. But just like in improv class I am committed to the scene. Accept, say yes, and move the action forward. Ms. Plunkett and the sappy teen angst group is taking away my edge. It must be. I can't believe I am saying this stuff to Ms. Clayton just because LOLA, of all people, said to. Aaand Look at this Kevin nonsense. Hmmmmm. I wonder if he decided on a time for the party.

"Addie. Ms. Sinclair, are you with us? Can you repeat what I said about high and low pressure systems?"

"Sunshine and rain, in that particular order."

And the bell for the end of class rings.

Ohmigawd. What have I gotten myself into this time?

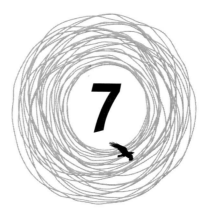

Lola catches up to me after class just as I am heading into the drama room. Lindsay is not with her, thank goodness, because I don't think I would be able to not stare at her and her newly leathered self.

"Sinclair," barks Lola. "I can help you get the Skywatch guy to come to our Geo class. He's a friend of my dad. And, um, actually, he's at our house right now. I will organize for him to be here next class. You will be some kind of hero to Ms. Clayton. I can hardly wait to see the look on your, oh actually, her face. It'll be magic, I swear."

"Thanks, Lola. I wasn't even serious. I was just trying to dodge a detention bullet. I can't believe you are helping me out with this. What's in it for you?" I look at her with a combination of admiration and fear on my face. This gesture of goodwill is making me rather suspicious. I always get sucked into stuff I don't want to get sucked into.

"Nothin' really. I just appreciate a good j….Hey Brooke, wait up. Seeya Sinclair." And with that Lola disappears into the river of kids streaming to next class.

What is this all about? I wonder. Oh well. Another day another inexplicable random event.

I notice the drama class is gathered around the call back list for the major production of the year. Bram Stoker's Dracula. I auditioned for the part of Lucy last week. Me and eleven other girls. I don't care if I don't get the part. I would be happy just to have any role. It's rare that someone in tenth grade would get a lead.

"Addie, did you see, did you see? You and Lola are called back for the part of Lucy." Misty Talbot, cheer squad member, squeals and reveals, breathless and chirpy.

Really? Ohmigawd! Me and Lola? Lola? Really? I had no idea she had auditioned. Hey. Hmmmmm. Wait a ridiculous minute. This is a very interesting development.

"Hey Misty. When was the call back list posted?" I ask.

"Yesterday after school. I don't know exactly but around four, I guess," she says.

" OOkay. Thanks."

Lola's goodwill is now something more than random. What exactly is she up to?

Ohmigawd. I am on the call back for the part of Lucy. Ohmigawd. This is so amazing and unbelievable at the same time. Oh wow. Oh man. Ohmigawd.

2:45 announces itself and Silverwoods Secondary burps its students out onto the streets and sidewalks. I wait for Sig under the plum tree at the end of the teachers' parking lot. I have a lot to talk about on our walk home today.

"Ya know Sig, this was a good day for a Tuesday considering it started out so sucky. Giant bad dreams gave way to a giant wish coming true. Well not completely true. I still have to audition again on Thursday for the part of Lucy and I have to compete for the role with Lola but hey I made it this far. And you know what? If I really want the role I will get it. I will prepare like a fiend for the next couple of days and voila. Lucy is mine."

Sigge smiles at me.

"You do remember that Bernerd is Dracula don't you?"

Hearing Sigge say this gives me goosebumples.

Is this why I am strangely driven to get this role? Impossible. Completely- no. Definitely not. Nu-uh. Nope. Negatory. Ix-nay.

"Yup. I remember. But I think I am inspired by the spirit of competition, Sig. Me-O vs Lola-O. May the best pale girl win!"

Win what exactly? I will segue away from this minefield.

"So Sig. What exactly have you organized for our Saturday night daring-do?"

" Well Add, I have a blanket, some sage for smudging, garlic garlands, organic, from Peter's Organic Garlic World on Hornby Island, some extra polaroid film, a tripod, a thermos for herbal tea, and the best most wonderful thing of all, Bernerd has secured us some serious transportation."

"I was hoping so because we have a lot of stuff to carry and the three of us on his scooter would be impossible. I have some lavender oil, a small container of smelling salts in case one of us faints, binoculars, tracing paper, a bunch of colored pencils, invisible ink, some notebooks, a history book about St. Andrews on the Red, and a map of the graveyard." I say matter of factly.

" Besides tea we have nothing to eat, Addie. I know this is supposed to be a coyote research project but it is also a picnic. What kind of treats would be perfect? And what is the lavender oil for?"

"I don't know. It smells nice and it's supposed to be relaxing. I am kinda expecting us to be a little anxious and nervous so I am taking precautions. And about food. Why don't we make some witch finger cookies and take them with us and some pumpkin muffins and a bowl of worms and dirt? As long as we don't bring food that looks like fluffy bunny coyote deliciousness I think we will be okay."

"Mmmm. Worms and dirt. I haven't had that in years. It's perfect. Ohmigawd. You know what else I am going to bring?" Sigge is suddenly breathless. "I am going to bring the graveyard scene from Hamlet. We will take turns reading it. I am getting chills just thinking about this. It is going to be such serious but fun, fun."

I just love Sigge. She will take any opportunity to become an artistic creepy scholar.

"So Sig. I am curious. What kind of transport does Bernerd have for us? Is he bringing the ever-faithful square but safe Volvo dad wagon?"

"Well Addie let's just say that I won't say. It's a surprise. A very appropriate surprise, all pending plays and events considered. I am really wound up for this Addie. This is going to be one remarkable weekend. One we will talk about for years to come."

"Do you want me to run in and get the lavender oil for you Sig?" I say and wink.

"L O L, not. Talk to ya later." And off she toddles, home.

8

Okay okay okay. Got to get this straight. What did she say?

2550 Tamarack Loop. 2550 Tamarack Loop. 2550 Tamarack Loop. 2055 Tamarack Loop. 2055 Tamarack Loop. 2505 Tamarack Loop. 2505 Tamarack Loop. 2255 2005 2502 Tamarack Loop. Nonononononononononon. You've got to think, stupid, think. **Think, THINK, Think!** Okay. 2550 Tamarack Loop. 2505 Tamarack Loop. 2055 Tamarack Loop.

Shit.

She didn't say.

"Candles? Black and white?"

"Check."

"Sage? BBQ Lighter?"

"Check and Check"

"Crystals?"

"Yep. Amethyst bracelet AND rose quartz necklace. You can never be too protected, Addie. And for Bernerd, amethyst cufflinks."

"Cufflinks? Does Bernerd have cuffs on his t-shirt?" I am having weird fashion visions.

"No Silly. This is a formal picnic investigation. He's wearing sleeves with French cuffs." Sigge tilts her head to the side and looks at me as if this is the most ridiculous question I have ever asked.

"That'll be some outfit! Only sleeves with French cuffs and cufflinks. Bernerd must be getting his fashion tips from my Dad! Eww." Once I start teasing Sigg it's really hard to stop.

"Addie, please. If you aren't going to take this seriously you are going to have to stay in the car the whole night. And if you aren't going to take this seriously we might forget something and who knows what might happen to us if we forget our safety supplies. How would I explain to your mom that you have disappeared into thin air because you forgot your amethyst bracelet?"

I am so intent on listening to Sigge that I am deaf to the sound of Lola and Lindsay marching across the cafeteria toward us. I am rather leery of Lola at the moment, considering that she is my "Lucy" competition and that Lindsay is Lindsay and everything, so I am less than happy to see the two of them. However, considering that Lola is helping me out with the meteorologist in the classroom I'll humour them.

"What are you two discussing so intently? And what is this? Give me that!" Lola grabs my list off the cafeteria table.

"Hey. Give that back Lola. That's private ya know!" whines Sigg.

"That's private ya know!" mocks Lola. " I never took you for a sniveller, Baxter. Snap out of it." Lola snaps her fingers under Sigge's nose. See? This is the nasty Lola.

"I never took you for a Cher wannabe, Lola." I stand up and assert myself into the conversation with a little more shoulder than I should.

"Hah. Good one Sinclair. Ya got me. Now let me have a good look at this shopping list. Lola holds the list up and pretends she is adjusting spectacles, on her nose. She starts to read as if this is a dramatic recitation. She is projecting our list in a fake British accent.

"CANDLES? SAGE, ROSEMARY AND THYME…?

Everyone in the cafeteria turns and looks to see who is speaking. Good grief. So much for not drawing attention to ourselves.

"Ya know ladies, this list makes me think that you guys are up to something rather witchy. The only thing missing is eye of newt and toe of frog!" Lola sneers and says,

"Whatta ya think, Zee?" as she hands off the list to her faithful new minion. "Zee" snickers as she reads the list. Lindsay has morphed into "Zee" it seems. She's way cooler, I guess, without the LINDS.

"Very Harry P. and cohorts. Very elementary, school that is! Bwahaha!" Lindsay snorts and wads the paper up into a ball and throws it at me. It bounces off my forehead and lands in a pool of salad dressing on my plate. 'Zee' and Lola link arms and snort themselves into the back corner of the cafeteria.

Sigge and I are looking very pathetic right this moment and it's not a look I want to cultivate.

"Sigge. What is the matter with us? We have never been so lame. I swear the one casting a weakness spell was Lola. Did you see that? Did you see Zee? Zee. Ohmigawd. What a ridiculous nick-name. Sigge?"

"Yeah? Oh. Sorry Addie. I know, right? Ridiculous. And look over there. That's what distracting me. The two of them look like a couple of crows on a wire, cawing and cackling. Fascinating coupling, that. I wonder what kind of stew they are brewing."

"Listen Zee. We've got to figure out what they are up to. I have got to jangle the nerves of that Sinclair competition. I really want to be Lucy. Tomorrow will be a good start but that is one interesting list. I wonder what it all means. What could they want with all that stuff?"

"That's easy Lola. It's almost Halloween. They are probably having a party or something. Whatever it is it's stupid and silly. Just like them. Forget about the list."

"You underestimate them Zee. They are very interesting adversaries."

"Adversaries? What are you talking about? They are immature high school girls. End of their story. So where is your dad and his band playing tonight and can we go?"

"They are playing at Vital Signs but I don't want to go. That place is a dump. It smells like beer and puke. I need to run lines tonight anyhow. Want to help me memorize?"

"I would rather go watch The Persuaders than help you memorize Dracula stuff. Come on Lola, please," begs Lindsay. "How else am I going to take a rock star to Prom if I never meet one?"

"Zee listen. Those guys are ancient. They are almost forty. They sleep all day and hang out in dark scuzzy bars all night. They are my extended family so you cannot take my father or any one of his goofy bandmates to Prom. So knock it off alright. Is it me or my dad and his band that you like?"

"When you put it that way, um, yech. And I like hangin' with you. So yeah, I will help you run lines."

"Excellent. You won't be sorry. I will let you in on a little somethin' somethin' that is going down tomorrow and I'll see if I can get my dad to let us backstage for the Persuaders weekend show. They are always better than Wednesday night gigs anyhow. Plus we need to get you some real leather before I take you anywhere. See ya tonight, Lind – ZEE. I've got to get to Math. Bye."

"Sweet. See you later Lola. I'm gonna meet me a rock star."

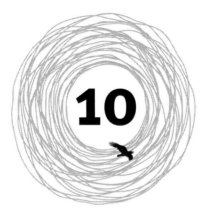

10

It's finally Thursday and Mr. Rod Rivers is joining us for Geography courtesy of Lola Lambert. She called me last night to remind me that she had made all of the arrangements and that Mr. Rivers would definitely be attending our class. She said he was happy to share his vast meteorological experience with mere peons. I am not sure he really said that but I am so glad that Lola was able to get him to come to our class on such short notice and to bail me out of a really uncomfortable situation. Scoring brownie points with Ms. Clayton is a bonus too! I hope that Rod makes weather "come alive" for our class. Or failing that at least conjure some clear skies for Saturday's midnight picnic and the full orange harvest moon. This has been the craziest, most busy week that I have had in a long time. Busy good, though. But I hope that Kevin gets back to me soon. Once rehearsals start I am not going to have too much time for him or party planning or anything else. Notice the confidence? I, me, Addie Sinclair, will be Lucy in Silverwoods Secondary School's production of Bram Stoker's

Dracula, as of tonight. The call back is right after school and I am prepared like never before. Look out Lola. Hmmm. LOL suddenly takes on a way new meaning.

But first things first: according to Lola I am to meet Mr. Rod Rivers with Miss Clayton at the front foyer of the school at 8:30 am. This is really nerve wracking. I have to hang out with Ms. Clayton and meet Mr. Rod Rivers. At least I get to take some of the credit for getting Mr. Rivers here. Yay! But even still,wobbly knees. How often does one get to meet a real local celebrity weather person?

In honour of this event Sigge made me and Ms. Clayton and Mr. Rivers matching turquoise bejewelled t-shirts that say "Lightning Rod Rivers is our Homeboy". It's a nice color but a rather cheesy saying. Ms. Clayton thought they were cute and well, here we are, standing at the front door, in our t-shirts, sparkling and waiting.

And waiting.

It's almost nine o'clock and Mr. Rivers has not appeared. I have a very sick stomach all of a sudden. Ms. Clayton is looking at me like I am a pathetic liar loser. I wonder if my trust in Lola Lambert is horribly misplaced.

"We should probably get back to class Addie. It looks like Mr. Rivers had a weather emergency and couldn't make it." Ms. Clayton looks truly disappointed and I feel just miserable.

"Do you want me to stay just a little longer maybe? If he is delayed we don't want him to feel unwelcome and lost." I ask in my most sucking up voice.

"Well okay, Addie. Seven more minutes and if he doesn't show up come back to the classroom please. We have wasted enough time for today." Ms. Clayton walks toward her room without a backward glance. I wonder if her t-shirt feels really heavy too.

I hear phones ringing in the main office. I hear dishes and pots clanging in the cafeteria. I hear kids' ipods thumping. I am paying attention to all of the noises around me as a distraction from this huge embarrassing moment that seems to be bleeding all around me. My cheeks and ears are on fire. My feet are pinned to the floor. My eyes are focussed on the front doors. I am willing Mr. Rod Rivers to materialize. There is a firm hand on my shoulder. I spin around and hope it is Mr. Rivers.

It's not. It's Joyce.

"Dammit, Joyce. Not only did you scare the living daylights out of me but you are not Mr. Rod Rivers." I bark.

Joyce is the secretary at the front desk of the school and I just kind of swore at her. If this were any other day I would be hugging her because she is the sweetest person and has the best Rapunzel hair ever. But now she is giving me the hairiest of evil eyes and would refuse a hug if I offered her one.

"Excuse me? What did you just say Ms. Sinclair? I am not sure that I heard you correctly." Joyce asks me politely.

"Oh, um, I said I am really truly sorry for barking at you and I really didn't mean it and I hope you can remember that I am not really that disrespectful most days and oh Hi Joyce. Did you need me for something?" Running all my words together has helped me in the past. Let's see how it works today.

"Ms. Clayton rang. She says you should go back to the class-room now. I didn't mean to startle you Addie but watch your mouth." Joyce smiles and heads back into the office.

See? She's completely lovely.

Well I guess Mr. Rod Rivers is not coming. This day had such promise and now, not so much. If I was smart I wouldn't go back to class and save myself the embarrassment but Ms. Clayton is expecting me and it is not as if she didn't see me this morning. Jeez. I can't win.

As I round the corner at the end of the hall I hear a commotion coming from Ms. Clayton's room. I see lights flashing as if photos are being taken and people are shrieking and laughing. Maybe he did make it after all. Maybe Mr. Rod Rivers came in the back door. Maybe that's why Ms. Clayton called me back to class. I so hope so.

I am one classroom away and I see "Zee" stick her head out of the classroom door.

"Shhhh. She's coming." She whispers.

This does not feel right but here I go, into the classroom, one foot in front of the other.

At the front of the room is a cluster of kids surrounding Mr. Rod Rivers. Ms. Clayton is sitting at her desk filing her nails and Lola and Lindzee are beaming really crazy smiles in my direction. Sigge is pale as a ghost and hiding her eyes.

When I am, at last, noticed, Jason Keble blurts, "Hey Addie come and get your picture taken with Rod. He's been waiting for you!"

The crowd around Rod disperses and I can see that Mr. Rod Rivers is somewhat less than alive. He is a life-size, life-like photo cut-out of his lovely self and he is wearing a pink hibiscus

Hawaiian lei and a rather European silver spandex bathing suit. This must have been taken before he was Channel Six's Skywatch weather guy. I am not completely sure this is the image they want to project into our fair city but he's got great abs.

The class is laughing at me as I take my place beside cut-out Rod. I drape my arm around his cardboard shoulder and plant a kiss on his paper cheek. There is no point wilting into the background. There is no point trying to hide. Camera-phones click and I am almost smiling.

11

"Miss Sinclair? May I see you for a brief moment please?" Ms. Clayton requests my presence as the rest of the class files out of the classroom. Sigge lags behind, waiting.

"Sure." I say. "Sigge don't wait for me. You might be late for Bio."

"Are you sure Addie? Actually?" I nod her away. I have got to deal with this myself. Poor old Sig got dragged into this crazy idea because of me so I might as well let her off of the hook.

" What can I do for you Ms. Clayton?" I ask with way more confidence than I feel. I know she is going to lay into me about this unfortunate misadventure with Mr. Rivers. I deserve it. I should have known better than to trust Lola and her minion Lind-Zee. I am lame.

"That was some stunt, Addie. Perfectly orchestrated actually. That thing we did, waiting at the front door, then you sauntering into class late after the whole Rod Rivers thing had been set up, not to mention the t-shirts. Well, all of that was brilliant. I hope you're happy . I am not sure what your intention was, whether you wanted to embarrass me or whatever, but oh my, that was HILARIOUS! Hah! You sure fooled me. I thought for sure that Rod Rivers was really coming. Well done."

Okay. This is weird. This is not what I expected from Ms. Clayton.

"Truthfully, I actually thought he was coming! I didn't want to embarrass you, I was just trying to avoid Wednesday school. I, too, was disappointed that he didn't show up. I didn't want to let you down. I actually contemplated not coming back to class but you knew I was here and I am walking a really fine line attendance-wise this year already, so that's why I came back to class and…."

"It's true Ms. Clayton." Sigge jumps into the conversation from outside the door. "I would have never made those t-shirts if we didn't think Rod Rivers was really going to make it to our class."

" That's quite a re-entrance Sigge." Ms. Clayton stifles a smirk. "So, tell me then. What happened girls? Why did you think he was actually coming? I noticed you were looking rather pale during Rod River's unveiling Sigge, but I attributed that to the fact that Addie had something to do with this. Did you think she was going to get into trouble?"

"Well she shouldn't." Sigge defends me. "The only thing she should get into trouble for is being a little too trusting and gullible, like she already has. It's a hazard of Ms. Plunkett's group. I am sure you know all about that. Anyway, it wasn't really Addie's fault. It was...."

"Sigge it doesn't matter now does it?" I say through clenched teeth and a hip check to her thigh. "It's over, I am embarrassed but alive and I have learned to check my sources. So, an event like this will never happen again. Trust me. NEVER." *Lola may be many things but I am certainly not going to throw her under a bus. Imagine what she would do to me if she thought I was a rat.*

"It was just a bit of a surprise that you wanted to organize this, and truthfully Addie, I was thankful he didn't show and, I'm actually not the least bit surprised. We used to date in university. I haven't seen him in years. I used to call him the 'Late' Mr. Rivers." Ms. Clayton blushes at this revelation and turns to write some notes on the white board. "And I think they used a body double for that cut-out. He never used to look like that!"

I look at Sigge with saucer eyes. She pretends to stick her finger down her throat and gag. This is one weird revelation.

"Ms. Clayton. Could you write Mr. Wade a note to let him know that we were talking to you and not loitering in the halls and stuff?" I beg. "Please?"

"Of course, ladies. Great bejewelling, Sigge, by the way." With that bon mot we are handed a note and shown the door. Ohmigawd.. The things that you learn.

"Did you see me jump into the room, Addie. It was a perfect cape moment but I was cape-less. I was swooping to save you. Did you see?" Sigge is impressed with herself. So am I actually but almost revealing Lola as the instigator of this whole event annoys me. And I can't afford to be annoyed. I have an audition call back. I cannot be flustered. I am the river. Anxiety runs through and away from me.

"Sigge. Are you sure you aren't really a superhero? You have the moves and the investigative tools and a mind that is so inquisitive that you could be the next Darkside Avenger, saving floundering high school girls from themselves and ghosts at historical haunting sites!" I am blathering as we walk toward our biology class.

"That was some run-on sentence Sinclair. What historical haunting site? What ghosts, What gives girls?" Lola lunges into our conversation.

What is it with people today? First Sigge leaping into the room, now Lola leaping into the conversation, uninvited I might add.

"Might this creepiness have something to do with your purloined list? Hmmmmm?"

Sigge shoots me a "reveal nothing" hairy eye-ball squint.

"No Lola it does not. What it does have to do with is ah, well, um, me preparing to play Lucy. You remember that we have a call-back today. I was throwing myself into the haunted essence of the character, as I am sure you have as well. I hope to see you at the finalized cast list tomorrow morning. May the best Lucy win. Break a leg, Lola!"

See? I can be the calm, unflappable river if I want to.

"TTFN Sinclair, Baxter. Oh hey, Sigge. Now that you have the two potential Lucy's standing right in front of you, and knowing

Dracula as well as you do, just from looking at the two of us who, just who, do you think is the worthiest Lucy?

Okay now that is testing my riverdom.

"Tres unfair question, LL. Only the Count knows for sure…."

"Come on Sigge." I say as I pull her elbow away from Lola. " Let's jump down the stairs and see if we can get some hang-time. Superheroes all have gravity defying hang-time. Let's fly girlfriend, bio is waiting." We speed walk toward the stairs and leave Lola in a small cloud of very un-twinkly dust.

"Zee, text me. The weird sisters are conspiring."

I really wonder what they are up to. Candles, sage, crystals, bbq lighter, stuffed rabbits, historical landmarks and ghosts: it is a creepy and eclectic list. There is something more to this than just play preparation. Sinclair is good, seemingly unflappable. The Rod Rivers debacle hardly shook her. I have underestimated her. I really want this part. Count Bernerd is H-O-T."

12

Mr. Noble, our drama teacher, paces as he thinks. Back and forth: left to right: right to left: backwards and forward: it's really annoying and it makes me nervous. Today he adds head shaking and mumbling to his repertoire. These two new qualities have amped up the tension in the room. Lola and I sit on the edge of the stage and watch. I can't help but swing my feet and fidget with my earrings. I clear my throat to remind Mr. Noble that we are still here and he is not alone.

Mr. Noble stops mid-pace. He casts his eyes to the ceiling, places his thumb and forefinger on either side of his chin, heaves a great sigh, and resumes his walk. When he gets to the furthest corner of the drama room he turns around and looks at the two of us with very wide and tortured eyes that seem to be floating in the darkness. He strokes his goatee and adjusts his maroon turtleneck. His disembodied voice floats toward us on the dead silence of the room.

"Ladies. Yes, you are ladies. What inspired performances from both of you! What a complete and utter disaster for me! The distinct qualities that each of you possess, that you bring to my vision of the ethereal Lucy are wonnnn-derful. Would they were all in the same person, at the same time, combined, twinned like the strands of DNA that make us who we are. Oh my! Both of you are ivory pale, moon- faced girls who reflect light into the character of Lucy; and both of you would be lures to the likes of a character, tortured as he is, like Dracula..."

Lola and I look at each other and simultaneously roll our eyes. Mr. Noble is lost in his own voice in the back dark corner of the drama room.

"...and with those thoughts I will leave you. I must contemplate, carefully the character ramifications of casting either of you into this most delicate part. I must consult with my Count Dracula. I must let you go and await the decision that will be posted Monday morning."

"What?" Are you kidding us? Are you serious? Are you nuts? Monday, Sir? We have to wait all weekend for your decision? We thought it would be tomorrow morning. Ohmigawd sir. Really? Actually? Oh man. I can't believe this. You are torturing us!" I spout.

As soon as this falls out of my mouth I could kick myself. Out of the corner of my eye I see Lola smiling serenely. She sits, wide-eyed, innocent, hanging on every word of the master, while I, on the other hand, am ranting and raving like some moon-mad lunatic. I am something less than ethereal and moon-like. *DAMMIT. Definitely not the river.*

"That will be all, Lola. Ms. Sinclair." There is a sudden edge to Mr. Noble's voice that feels sharp and knife-like and I have a pain right where my heart should be.

"So, Mizz Sinclair. Have a nice weekend. See ya at the posting on Monday. What are you up to? I am going to watch some vintage b-movies, Little Shop of Horrors perhaps, keep me in the spirit of things. You?" Lola chirps wide-eyed innocently as we leave the drama room.

I am rattled. I am off-track; a boulder has entered the river. I am not thinking when I say...

"Picnic," and shuffle my way toward my locker.

"Have fun, sucker." Lola calls to my back.

What the what? What was that for? I should have thrown her under the bus. That wasn't very nice. Sucker? Me? Oh Man. I shouldn't have popped off. I blew it. No Lucy for me I betcha. This is going to be one loooooong weekend. I have got to get home. I need my room, my moon, my friend.

"Hey Mom! I'm home. Home at last, home at last, thank-God I am home at last."

"Oh hey dear. I am in my office, folding laundry. How was your day? What did you learn?" Mom yells from the laundry room.

"My day was a giant knot in my stomach. I learned I am an ass. I need to lie down. See you at dinner." I say rather matter- of-factly.

"I can hardly wait for pasta too dear. The day has gone too fast!"

I don't think she heard an actual word I said. Oh well. It's nesting time in the Addie zone.

It's quiet and warm. The hum of the clothes dryer and the scent of fabric softener fills the air. It will be a couple of hours before my dad gets home from work and the job of dinner creation begins. Tonight it's Italian sausage penne pasta with caprese salad. Mom's favourite things to cook and assemble. Until then though I am going to hang upside down on my bed, like a bat, an homage to Dracula if you will. I will look out my window and wonder what's going on in my head. I grab a glass of water, a honeycrisp apple and a box of rosemary crackers and haul them up the stairs to my room. My comforter on my bed is calling me. It is lumpy and cushy and warm. I will wrap myself up and turn myself around and create a nest where I can contemplate the next step in this Addie journey. I will drape myself over the end of my bed, I will locate my darling moon-like friend and voila think –time. The street lights have just turned on and the smell of autumn wood fires insinuates itself into my room.

"Hi Moon. There you are. So here's the thing. One minute I am happy and cheerful the next I am cranky and irritable. The unexpected sets me off. When I expect stuff and it doesn't happen I snap. When I am teased I snap. I am an emotional elastic band, apparently snapping at will. I long for some stasis. Emotional boredom is what I am looking for I think. What do you

66

think, Moon? Do you think too much has happened in the last couple of weeks? Will I ever be completely capable of managing drama without crazy rearing its head? Help me find an explanation for my rude behaviour today. First I yapped at Joyce and then Mr. Noble. Who next? Oh no, Moon. I wouldn't ever consciously yap at you. You are the only true constant in my life. And look at this picture, this is you last night. I found it in the paper. Aren't you beautiful? I have never in my life seen your cheeks so round and shiny and the most incredible shade of cheese orange ever. Sigge and Bernerd and I are looking forward to hanging out with you tomorrow night. You will be resplendent in your harvest best and we will be waiting for coyotes and ghosts. We all will have a wonderful time. You know of course that I am only telling you this because I really can't stand the thought of thinking about the Lucy scenario. What if I don't get the part. What if Lola is the chosen one? I have worked so hard and so long to get this and to have it snatched away because I snapped. Wow. That would be a serious life lesson now wouldn't it? Healing is hard, Moon. I already know that. I just want things back to a Sinclair version of normal. You know, just crazy velour fashions and olive green appliances? Things that should make you loopy but are really like hugs? I am thankful for the recent undrunk somewhat sane mother scenario. Don't misinterpret Moon, but this is a version of normal that I am not completely used to yet. " Time will unravel this not I" to quote Twelfth Night and Shakespeare. I just wish I wasn't so snappy, so anxious, so tightly wound. Why don't we have a little nap and sleep on all of this okay?"

13

Sigge is at the door. Awfully, freakin' early for a Friday. We start classes late on Fridays. We don't have to be at school until ten, not like the usual eight thirty start time.. It's only eight o'clock and showered and shiny Sigge is here begging to be let into my kitchen. I am still a groggy Addie. I didn't get a restful sleep. I am so sad about blowing up at the end of the audition. I am so angry that Lola called me a sucker and she proved it twice in one day. It's nice to have Sigge here to trust.

"Let me in!" Sigge bangs on the window. It's a fabulous Friday and I come bearing treats. Look at this! It's a photo of the moon! It was in the paper yesterday, I brought it for you, for your moon. Look at how big and orange it is! Imagine the kind of light it is going to shine on us tomorrow night when it's completely full. Addie I am so "over the moon" about our picnic I can hardly stand it. I know you're upset about yesterday but we still have our picnic. Mr. Noble has to know that you are the best Lucy and Lola is not.

Cheer up my transparent friend. Get dressed and I will take you for breakfast before school starts. Come on get dressed and let's go go go! Does your mom want to come with us?"

"What? That's random. My mom? I don't think so. I haven't seen her this morning yet. Where are we going and how are we going to get there?" I grumble.

Come to think of it just where is my mom this morning? She has been up and bustling about the kitchen every morning for the past couple of weeks. Hey wait. She wasn't up yesterday morning either. Hmmm. This is an interesting and thought provoking observation that I really don't want to dwell on right now. There is not enough time in the day for any more scary behaviour from members of my family.

"Oh did I mention that the moon picture is only part of the surprise? Bernerd is waiting outside for us. That's part two." Sigge smiles as she drops Bernerd into the conversation like a hot potato.

"Is this the transportation reveal, Sigge? Ahhh. I get it. I will get my clothes on. Two seconds and I will be right back."

I take the stairs two at a time to my room; there I throw myself into something stretchy and cosy, brush my teeth, wash my face and wind the ginger feathers of my hair into a messy bun. Off I go into the Baxter universe.

I jump from the top of the stairs and land my cape-less landing with style and balance. Sigge applauds appropriately and pushes me toward the door.

"Close your eyes, Addie. I want this to be a complete and total surprise. Don't worry I will guide you out of the door." Sigge takes me by the elbow and leads suddenly- blind me onto the front step.

As I step onto the front porch I can hear the purring of a car engine in the cul de sac. An "arooga" horn blows and I open my eyes to see the most wondrous monstrosity of a car. Let me amend that. Hearse. Lime green and black really stretchy hearse.

"Hah! That is the most amazing thing I have ever seen Sigge." Hurry. I can't wait to get in it. Omigawd it is so cool." I am dragging Sigge across the yard toward the car. "Bernerd! When did you get this. This is such a fabulous ride! It is totally crazy, and completely you. I love the color. Sigge why didn't you tell me it was the most awesome – est thing ever? This is the most perfect vehicle for our weekend escapade. Now I know why you didn't tell me. You save all the best information until I really need it. Wow Bernerd. This is great. Are you completely loving it? You must sling a whole lotta pizza."

"Actually, to be honest, no one really wants hearses, so it was cheap," admitted Bernerd, his smile as wide as the dashboard. "That is how I was able to customize it. I saved money on the initial cash outlay. Black button-tuck leather seats, lime green velvet curtains, blue plastic roses, red toss cushions, a kind of homage to Dracula, and this very groovy chain-link steering wheel. I can't afford an apartment just yet, so this is my new home on wheels. Whattaya think?"

"It is quite something, Bern. Very impressive and it doesn't even smell bad."

"I know, right. It's funny you would say that, Addie. That was the first thing I thought of when I saw it for sale. I figured it was going to smell like death or something. Not that I know what death smells like or anything so when I got into it and it was clean laundry fresh I bought it."

"Bernerd, Addie, look at me," giggles Sigge as she lies straight out in the back of the hearse with a blue plastic rose between her teeth and her arms crossed over her chest.

" Except for the rose Sigge, you look exactly like the corpses in all those old ancient scary movies." I say as Bernerd pulls the car away from the curb. "Where are we going for breakfast?"

"How about the Star Grille, kids?" Bernerd offers. "I have coupons!"

The Star Grille is way cute. It is in the park right next to the conservatory across from a bronze statue of a giant ox pulling a cart. That may not sound cute but it really is and I have been dying to see it.

"Bernerd, Sigge this is so great. I have been desperate to come here since it opened. This is perfect. What a great way to start a late day."

I feel special and privileged and very cool right now. I am with my best friends and it feels so good. There is a comfort here that I never felt with Lindsay. They know me. We are from the same bolt of cloth.

The Star Grille has a navy blue ceiling with stars and planets suspended from it. There are midnight blue velvet curtains that drape diagonally across the windows, elegant and sophisticated to my mind, and some of the most beautiful serving people I have ever encountered. I should have worn something more than a hoodie and sweatpants.

We are shown to our table by "Shelby". She has great teeth and a very simple form-fitting black dress. The table is festooned with a gold metallic table cloth, white and gold china, gold cutlery and a single white Calla lily. It is rather overwhelming all this beauty first thing in the morning. There is no smell of burnt toast or two hour old coffee. Everything here is perfect.

"What is the occasion you guys? Why so way fancy? I expected a bun on the run." I ask, curious.

"AAAAAAAAAAAAAAAAAA. Bernerd I can't stand it. I have to tell her. Look at her little face. She is so clueless. Addie. You are LUCY! YOU GOT THE PART!" shrieks Sigge.

"You have got to be kidding me. For really and for true? Actually? How do you guys know this? I will reserve my shrieking until you clarify how you know." I say stunned and amazed that this could be happening.

"Well last night, when I was rehearsing with Mr. Noble," explains Bernerd, "He told me about his Lucy dilemma. He told me that until you and Lola came in for your call backs that he knew that he was going to cast Lola. But then when you popped off and demonstrated a devilish side to your personality, he had to change his mind because that personality transformation is exactly what happens to Lucy in the play! You could not have rehearsed it better. Addie, your unpredictable and rather explosive crankiness has paid off! Congratulations our friend. This is your celebratory breakfast."

"Ohmigawdohmigawdohmigawd! I am so glad I am sitting down right now! I can hardly breathe. I thought for sure Lola was the one. I was so sure. Well she was the one but now she is not and Oh man, you guys, Thank-you so much for doing this.

You have no idea how wonderful you are. You are making my little heart throb with love. Thank-you so much." Tears dribble down my cheeks as I confess this.

"Our pleasure Ms. Adelaide Blanche Sinclair, the reigning Lucy du jour. Now let's order. I am famished." Bernerd hushes his grumbling stomach.

Okay. So I am Lucy. Yay! But that means that Lola is not. Not Lucy. Not in the play as Lucy. Not going to be happy. Not going to be happy with me especially. You know what. I can't worry about how she is going to react. It's no longer about her. It's about me now. I am Lucy. I earned that part, sorta. So Lola, so there.

"A round of giant baby apple pancakes for me and my friends, barkeep. And keep the coffee flowin'.

Bernerd is hilarious and generous and has great taste in vehicular transportation.

I am so loving him, er, this moment, right now.

"Okay, Zee. Let's think. Let's put this all together. Picnic blanket, black candles, sage, historical haunting site map, crystals, worms and dirt, giant bbq lighter. What do all of these things have in common? How are they connected? C'mon. Help me out here."

"Why are you so interested in what Addie and Sigge are up to, Lola? You've never been that interested in them and what they do before. It's just the Dracula thing and Hallowe'en stuff. Nothing more. Wait a minute. Does this have something to do with Bernerd? No way. Really? Bernerd? Actually, honestly, he is kinda cute. He's so different, so dramatic. He doesn't care about what anyone thinks. He's very independent. I like that actually. Independence is actually quite attractive don't you think, Lola? Lola? Are you listening to me?" Lindsay snaps as she slams the door to her locker.

"What's the date today Lindsay?"

"What? It's October 22. Why?"

"That's it! I figured it out. I know what they are up to. Do you know what tomorrow is Zee?"

"October 23?"

"Yup and it's the full moon. So follow me here Lindsay. At what nearby historical site would you have a picnic on the night of the full moon?"

"Probably that old church by the river on Highway 13."

"Yup." You guessed it. You are a genius. So that is their plan. A picnic at St. Andrew's on the night of the full moon. The list of stuff is protective gear so that they are kept safe from evil spirits. I knew they were up to something. How evil are you feeling these days Zee? Are you in the mood for some pre-Halloween fun?" Lola's eyes sparkle with anticipation.

"I guess so. But I will have to stay at your house if we are going to be out later than midnight otherwise I'll have some explaining to do. And wait a minute. Didn't you say we were going to go to a Persuaders gig? I really want to go to a show."

"Say yes to my plan and the gig is yours, Zee. But if you continue to whine, you are outta here."

"A duress yes," sighs Lindsay.

"This is going to be so much freakin' fun, Zee. This is the stuff of high school legend, a total night to remember. So come on. Let's get out of here now, before this really lame school day even starts. We have some planning and preparations to make. Our first stop is Summer Underground to get you a real leather skirt and second is Connie's Costume Corral for the finishing touches."

"What are you talking about? Are we ditching school?" Lindsay squeaks. " Really? Right now? Oh man this is so rock and roll. Connie's Costume Corral? That's a random fashion destination. But who cares. This is nerve-wrackingly awesome."

"Zee, we are about to secure ourselves places on Silverwoods High School Wall of Serious Capers. Let's get a move on."

Breakfast with Sigge and Bernerd was a delicious and nutritious way to start my day but I am still a little apprehensive about going into school, with the Lucy situation. I am such a sucky liar that Lola will know something is up because I won't be able to make eye contact with her. Plus I am so excited that I got the part that I will blab it at her as soon as I see her. I am doomed. I will lay low and try and avoid her. We don't have any classes together today so that makes things easier and I will run home for lunch and

"Excuse us, barging through." Lola and Lindsay snicker as they push their way past the three of us and the throng of other kids entering the school doors. "Exiting stage left."

I watch as the two of them run like wobbly crows across the track into Munday Park away from school into the trees, cackling the whole way. There is something creepy about their departure but it makes it so much easier to go to school today. No Lola. No lie. No problem.

"What's up with them?" asks Sigge. "Where are they going?"

"Never mind them, Sig. But hey, I just want to say, Bernerd, Sigge, thanks for the great morning. Fab way to start the day.

Food and friends. See ya later, at your house, Sigge. We'll get the supplies organized and color coded. Bye." I grin at Sigge and Bernerd, my smile complete with teeth. Right now there is nothing to lie about and I have the best peeps.

School is almost over before it starts. I love, love, love late Fridays.

"Now kids. I am off to the hot springs on a work retreat for a couple of days. You are responsible for the care and feeding of your father. He works the late shift tonight and should be home around midnight. Tomorrow remind him to eat or he won't leave his studio. Make sure you pry him away from the kiln. Bernerd, I have left some gas and laundry money on your dresser. You have to drive Sigge to her art class tomorrow morning and don't forget to pick up the dry cleaning. I left the claim ticket with the money. Sigge I made lasagne, it's in the fridge, and there are strawberries and spinach so you can make the salad for dinner tonight. Addie, it's nice to see you, and you are welcome to stay for dinner and for the night if you wish. But I have to go now. I want to get to Harrison before it is completely dark. It's a crazy highway." Mrs. Baxter reads from her list of things to tell her kids to do before she heads out the door. "Good bye my darlings. I will see you Sunday afternoon. Have a fun and safe weekend. Say hello to your parents Addie. Bye kids." Mrs. Baxter kisses both kids on their respective foreheads before she heads out the door.

"Bye Mom. Love you." Bernerd and Sigge chirp together. *Geez. Syrupy sweet and fuzzy warm people with no velour in sight.*

"Okay Addie," says Sigge as she takes the blue glass pan of lasagne out of the fridge and slides it into the oven, "what time should we leave tomorrow night?"

"I have to work until ten you guys, so we can't leave much earlier than ten thirty," interjects Bernerd.

"Oh right. I forgot you had to work." Sigge sighs. "Couldn't you have changed your shift? This is very important coyote research!"

"It's okay, Sigge. There is still a lot of time. How about we leave at 10:45? We can get there without rushing and we will still be there before midnight." I say with a patience I have never demonstrated before. "There would be no hearse without the job so, chill..."

Good Grief. Now I am defending Bernerd from Sigge. Highly unnecessary, highly un-me. This sappy behaviour has got to stop.

"Oddly enough Addie, you are right. I am so wound up I could just howl, or chew my own leg off in anticipation of our evening. Sorry Bern. I didn't mean to be yappy."

"Whatevs." Bernerd yawns.

"Ya know guys I am going to go home. If I am going to stay here tomorrow I think I'll hang out at home tonight. I should run my lines for next week anyway. I want to ensure that Mr. Noble doesn't regret his Lucy decision. See you ."

The door to the Baxter's house closes with a soft thud behind me and I feel like whistling myself home, but here's the thing. I hate the sound of whistling but it feels exactly like what I should do right now.

This has been one sweet, sweet day. A sweet whistling a happy-tune-to-the-moon kind of day.

15

I am so glad it is Saturday. Noon has come and gone and the afternoon is in full swing. I am rolling around in the comfort of my pink zebra comforter while the rest of my household is off at work or being extraordinarily silent. My window is open and the breeze is helping my curtains pretend to be flags. They gently wave their turquoise velvety sleeves at me, wishing me a fresh autumn hello. They draw my attention to the warmth of the sunshine and the serenity of my neighbourhood. Crispy leaves that refuse to let go of their tree's branches tickle the side of the house. I hear the scratching of twiggy fingers on the siding.

I stayed up way past midnight reciting and reviewing my lines. I feel pretty confident that I understand the character of Lucy. I hope it is an interpretation that Mr. Noble agrees with. Lucy is beautiful and tortured and seduced by the elegance and sophistication of the Count. She is naïve and easily led. She is every teenaged girl. How can I go wrong?

The idea of actually getting up is exhausting. I know I have to get over to Sigge's but my room smells so good and my blanket is so warm and my pillow is calling my name …if I just put my head down for a second and close my eyes and breathe in the silence and sunshine…

There are crickets chirping all around me. I am asleep in a golden field of flowering canola against a navy blue sky. Thunder is rolling in the distance. A sense of impending doom is spreading through my veins, there is a lightning flash and crackling much too close to me. More crickets, a whole herd of crickets: wait a minute, it's my phone I am not going to be hit by lightning, it's just my phone.

"Hello and thank-you." I breathe into the phone.

"Addie? Don't tell me you were still sleeping. It's four o'clock. You realize that you have to be over here in thirty minutes don't you. I have painted and made cookies, and cleaned and well done everything that you have not done today. Do you think that you could drag your sorry self over here and help us get ready? Geez." Sigge sighs.

She is awfully grumpy today.

"Judging from your mood maybe you should have slept a little longer yourself, missy. I will be over before you know it. Make a list of what you want me to do when I get there. We aren't even leaving for another six hours. So hold yer horses, bucko. I will save you from yourself." I try and make Sigge feel a little less angsty but until I get over there who knows if it has worked.

"Just hurry up, okay?" Sigge disconnects me without a good-bye.

Hmmm. I wonder what has gotten her shorts in a knot? Cranky is so unlike her.

I pull on my black jeans, black long sleeved t-shirt,and black and red striped socks. Then I tie on my black sneakers. I pull my hair into a ponytail with a red elastic. I insert subtle touches of colour that only I will know are there. Who knows why this is important to me tonight but it is. I wrap my black and white leopard-print scarf around my neck, grab my red and black polka dotted hoodie, my phone, my camera and my lime green backpack. This is going to be either the most scary and creepy night of all nights or it's going to be really fun and coyote insightful. I am not sure just exactly what we will do if there is a pack of marauding coyotes but hey, it's an adventure and we get to have a midnight picnic and drive out to an historical cemetery in a hearse. I can hardly wait. The anticipation is making me sweat. Ew.

I close the kitchen door behind me and the screen door closes itself. I don't need to lock them.. Mom is probably in the garage or in the back yard or napping and my dad will be home soon. He takes the bus home on Saturdays. Parking at the mall on the weekend is murder he says and it only takes him twenty minutes to get home anyway, so why should he torture mom? I think I mentioned I was going to stay at Sigge's tonight when I got home last night. Where else would I be? It's not as if the open door policy at the Dixon's is still in effect. I'll call home later. I aim myself toward the Baxters.

The Baxter's house is only four doors away. Our house is on the side of the circle right next to the sidewalk that connects to the cul de sac behind us. Their house is at the top of the circle. They have the biggest back yard. It's slice of pie shaped. They back onto an empty lot that is overgrown with blackberry brambles. A very delicious problem. Mrs. Baxter whips up blackberry muffins, and blackberry raspberry pie and makes a syrupy stuff that you pour over vanilla ice-cream. Yum.

Anyhow, I think it is karma that Sigge and I are friends. Our addresses have the same numbers in them, just in a different order. It's hilarious. We were destined to meet, if not through karma at least through numerology. When they moved in last March I was relieved and happy that some new kids moved into the cul de sac. Most of the families have lived here all of the kids lives. It's nice to have some new blood in the 'hood.

The hearse is backed into the Baxter's driveway and the back door of the hearse is open. Sigge is on her knees inside the carriage fluffing up the black suede shag rug that Bernerd has installed. She hums "Love Will Tear Us Apart" as she organizes our supplies and ensures the rug is so fluffy that it could swallow your feet up to your ankles. Bernerd has applied a pink magnetic skull and crossbones to the gas tank door. This mobile unit gets cooler all the time.

"It's about time you got here!" Sigge snaps. "Did you think you could just walk over and hop into the passenger seat without doing any of the work, Addie? Well, did you?"

Sigge has never spoken to me like this before, ever. I didn't think that she knew how to be snippy, but in the last couple of days she has been downright ornery. I wonder what's up.

"There's no need to stand there slack-jawed Adelaide. Grab a box. Find a dust cloth. Something, anything. Just do something."

"Now wait a little minute, Sig-knee. I don't know what bee is in your invisible bonnet, but what's, pardon the expression, bugging you? What have I done? Why are you so angry with me? I couldn't have come over any earlier, you weren't home, or don't you remember. It's not as if I am going to hang with your dad and shoot the breeze about the group home. What's got you so twisted? Had I known you wanted me to be here all day long keeping the home fires burning you should have let me know. You have been less than your lovely self for the past couple of days and if it is something that I have done, hey, let me know. And for the record, if there is something that I can help you with, I would love to help. You have always been there for me so..."

"Nada, nothing, nope, not one stupid, freakin' thing. Just hand me the microfiber duster."

Sigge can't even look at me. If I am not mistaken she seems like she is kinda, well, jealous.

"Sigge listen. I am going to go home. I can't do this if you are angry with me. It won't be any fun for any of us. I don't know what I have done. I don't know how to fix it if you won't talk to me. So, give me a call when you are ready. See ya. Bye. Have a nice life."

I am almost two houses home when I hear,

"Okay. Alright. I am ready to talk. Get back here would ya?" Sigge yells.

"Will you talk nicely to me?" I say with a smile in my voice. I can be so cheeky sometimes.

"Yes. Okay Addie. I need you to clear something up for me. I need to know if, if, if.."

"If what, Sig? Spit it out."

"If you are only friends with me because of Bernerd. That you aren't only friends with me because my brother is Dracula and in twelfth grade. That you think that by being friends with me that he will like you…."

"Did you hit your head on the side of the car, Sig? Are you suffering from a serious head injury? You are my friend because of you .You are one heck of an artist. You make me laugh. You have a great imagination and you like escapades like the one we might embark on tonight."

"What about Bernerd? Is it me, or is it him you really like?' Sigge snivels into the carpet.

"And you happen to have a brother who I will be acting with in the school production. He is a good actor. He is your brother. You are my friend. He is my friend. You guys are my rocks, my besties. I like you both. Nothing more than that my goofy fiend. So is that it? Are we good?"

"Yup. I just needed to hear you say it outloud, I guess, Addie. So you know what? There was another news report on the coyotes today. Now they are eating, get this, blue plastic roses that are left on grave sites. This morning, out at St. Andrews, there were hundreds of shredded blue plastic roses. Blue Roses were everywhere. The Historical Society is hysterical. The coyotes are running amuck. The police are baffled. They have set traps, but have caught nothing except fake blue roses. I can hardly wait to get out there."

16

The hearse is loaded with all of our gear. The only thing missing is Bernerd. It is 10:15 and Sigge and I are wound up. We think of songs to sing on our drive because we need to do something to pass the time. Forty-five minutes is a long time to be silent when you are not sleeping. I hope Bernerd had an interesting night at work. That at least will give us something to talk about.

"Can you believe how serendipitous it is that Bernerd has decked out his hearse with blue plastic roses. Do you think it could be a sign, Addie? Do you think we are destined to solve the mystery of St. Andrew's?"

"I truly don't know, Sigge. But what I do know is that my knees are getting really wobbly thinking about this. Look at the moon. It is huge and orange and a little scary looking don't you think? The fact that it has no light of its own yet is capable of being so bright and orange and full, and able to manipulate the tides and emotions, really speaks of its power, Sigge. I'm kinda scared just looking at it. This is nothing like my moon. Actually, now that I think about it, the moon is only part of the problem. I am really scared of coyotes. What are we thinking? Shouldn't we be leaving this problem to animal control people? We are three high school students with a flair for the dramatic. What do we know about catching wild animals and spirits?"

"There is no catching involved, Addie. Except on film of course. We are just there as witnesses to document the truth of the moment. We want to know all of our fellow creatures on our earthly plain. Coyotes or ghosts it doesn't matter. We are all in this together.

"Okay. Whatever you say, Sig."

I take comfort in the whirring sound of Bernerd's scooter engine as he enters the cul de sac.

"Ladies. Are you freakin' ready for an evening of fun and ectoplasmic emissions?" Bernerd says as he takes off his scooter helmet and parks the Vespa in the driveway. "I am so stoked to get this adventure underway that I've hardly been able to keep my delivery addresses straight. I see that you have packed the hearse with everything we could possibly need for a year of food and entertainment. This is good, so let me go inside the house to say hello and goodbye to dad, use the facilities, then let's get a move on."

"Did you hear about the blue roses at the cemetery, Bern. I just can't believe it. What an amazing coincidence!" Sigge yells as Bernerd enters their house from the garage.

"I did hear Sig." Bernerd pops his head around the door frame. "However, to my way of thinking, there is no such thing as coincidence. It is how it is meant to be."

Okay now kids. This is getting way too creepy.

17

I will start at the beginning and work my way around.
Work my way around. I will start at the first one and work my
way around.

It all looks the same and they are filled with fives. The
houses are all filled with fives...

2505?

2550?

2555?

All of them. I will start at the beginning and work
my way around. They have to be somewhere. She said

they were close by. This looks like it could be it. No lights by 11:00 seems a little early for them. One, two, three, four five, will this fish get out alive? Six, seven eight nine ten, whack him once then hit him again... Let me try the door. It's unlocked. Let's try the inside door. Open. Dark kitchen. Light on at end of hall. Quiet, quiet, hold breath, super freakin' quiet. Hey shhhh, what's that grinding sound? Stay close to the floor, follow the shadow, follow the sound. Wrong house. Wrong place. Wrong guy. Oh well. Just in case he wakes up later.

On my belly, on the floor, out the door, down the stairs, follow the shadow, close to the shrubs, dogs barking, dogs barking, stop in the shadow, dogs quiet, run to a shadow, run to a shadow, I am a shadow in the night. Run. Run faster. I see it. There it is. This is it. I know it. The scooter. Bernerd's scooter. This is it. Finally. Garage door code. 1234. Of course. It works. Into the shadow, into the light of the hallway, follow the light, follow the music, follow the music, is this really psycho killer? Follow the music, stay in the shadow of the wall, stay small in the hall, don't breathe, hold your breath, look around the corner, what do you see? **Now what? what do you want, what do you need, shit.** He's turned around. he sees me. Stay in the shadow grab a bowl, a bigger bowl, the biggest bowl, shit.

Now hit!

now **blood**...

No need to worry about the light,

grab and run,

and hide,

hide,

hide...

18

Except for the crunching of tires on gravel, all is silent, midnight blue. Bernerd switches off the headlights of the hearse as we enter the cemetery parking lot. It takes a while for my eyes to adjust to the sudden darkness. I am impressed with the depth of my fear. I had no idea how scared I could actually feel. I might just want to stay in the car with the doors locked under a blanket, invisible and quaking.

The television blue light illuminating the cemetery is cold and angular. It is not the warm bath of moonbeams that I feel in my room. The curve of the headstones slice the darkness, into a kaleidoscope of shattered grey and blue shadow. There seems to be no end to the way this silver cold light fractures my courage.

I hold my breath and scan the parking lot for coyotes. Thankfully there is nothing here but us. Sigge is alert and anxious for the fun to start. We are both quivering but for very different reasons.

The silence is thick, like furry ear muffs. I hear the blood coursing through my veins, my heartbeat thudding through my sweatshirt.

"Can you believe how much this looks like a horror movie set?" whispers Bernerd as he shifts the hearse into park. "Look at the mist. It is knee high! This is going to be so cool to walk through. Sigge, hand me the video camera. Addie switch your phone to video and Sigge will take footage of you with it as you move through the mist. I want to get as many angles and shots as possible. Even if we don't encounter the coyotes I want to document as much of this escapade as we can. I can feel a presence here can't you guys? It doesn't feel dead to me though. It feels very alive and electric."

Bernerd is chatting away in the best stage whisper I have ever heard. It is as if it's noon and not the dead of night in a graveyard. His eyes are shooting out sparks of excitement as he talks. He unlocks and opens the back door of the hearse to unload our supplies. Sigge is creeping around the car with her phone on camera, clicking pictures. I have my phone on video pointing at the ground and shaking like a leaf. I am so freaked out right now. What happens if we do see something? Omigawd this is creepy.

Out of the corner of my eye, over the wrought iron fence, I think I see something move.

"Um hey guys. Did you see that? Over there to my right. Behind that first headstone. I think I saw something . Seriously, I did."

"Okay, so did you point the camera in that direction? If you are too scared to look, at least let the camera record what you can't bring yourself to see." Sigge hisses under her breath. "We need good documentation of this event Addie. Don't let me down."

"This is so freaky, Sigg. Aren't you a little bit scared?" I ask. My breathing is shallow and I am feeling on the verge of a heart attack.

"Of course I am, Addie. Without this adrenalin I wouldn't feel as alive right now as I do. I am scared but it is so worth it."

"Shhhhh, you guys listen..." Bernerd hushes us.

I can hear the rustling of dried grass coming from the grave yard. My feet are suddenly clad in Frankenstein boots. I cannot move and I cannot breathe. I want to scream. I have the same feeling that I get on roller coasters. I want to cry, scream and vomit all at the same time. The sound is getting closer and I close my eyes. I don't want to see what is about to devour me.

"I know you are scared Addie, but hold up the phone!" Bernerd pleads. "I really would like to have footage of more than just the gravel and your sneakers."

I stick my left arm straight up in the air and move the camera around in the area where I think I hear something. My right hand is covering my eyes and my lungs are paralyzed.

"Okay, Addie. Listen to me very carefully." I hear Sigge say rather breathlessly herself. "Keep the camera in the air but point it down toward the ground..."

"But I thought Bernerd said..."

"Shhhhhhhh." Sigge cuts me off. "Just do as I say. Start to back up towards the car. Really slowly. Don't make any sudden moves."

"Ohmigawdohmigawdohmigawd. What is it Sigge?" I am moving slowly backwards toward the open side door of the car. The car seat hits me just behind the knees and I fall into the back seat. As I land my eyes snap open and I can see the offending noise maker waddle back into the darkness.

"Hah! Addie look. It's okay. It's just a skunk. It must have been attracted to your scarf!" giggles Sigge.

"I thought I was going to die, really. Omigawd Sigge. That was scary. You could have told me it was just a skunk."

"See, Addie. There was a logical explanation for the sound you were hearing. There is nothing here to scare us except our imaginations. So far. We know there are skunks here, so there must be other animals that are active at night. The sounds that we hear will be from animals and insects, for the most part anyway. I have never heard a ghost so I will attribute any strange noises that I hear to either you or Bernerd. And I didn't tell you it was a skunk because you probably would have screamed and it would have sprayed us and this evening would have ended sooner than we planned. Was that the presence that you felt, Bernerd."

"Oh probably, the excitement of being here is an entity in itself! This is so cool. I don't know why I haven't done this as a field trip before. Anyhow, let's find a place to set out all of our stuff. It is 11:45. Almost the witching hour."

"Don't say that Bernerd. You are going to scare Addie."

"I know! Addie I am a little surprised by your nervousness. Your daily self is so prickly that I didn't think that this spooky stuff would get to you. Appearances are definitely deceiving."

"Well, thanks for that Bernerd. I just have a finely tuned imagination that's all. I believe anything can happen so…So I am nervous, so what?" I shake a little as I say this.

"So nothing. You are, how you are, that's all. You are surprising at every turn." Sigge smiles at me and shoots a stink eye at Bernerd.

"Lindsay! If you are going to continue to giggle like that we are going to be discovered in no time. The point is to stay undetected until the very last moment. When the three of them are comfortable in their surroundings and they are least expecting to be scared. Just like us right now. So knock it off! I want this to work." Lola spits and hisses.

"I can't help it, Lola. Did you see her face? Addie is petrified. When she fell into the back seat I thought she was going to throw up. This is so ridiculously hilarious." Lindsay stifles herself.

"I must say though Zee, that your idea to come here last night was inspired! Throwing around all those shredded blue roses. Fabulous. Where did you get that notion? I am certainly liking how you think. You are definitely more of an equal than a minion."

"Thanks Lola. I don't know. Yesterday at breakfast my dad was talking about this news story that he had heard about coyotes and some cemetery. Apparently the coyotes attack the loved ones of the people buried in the cemetery. The animals seem to throw around blue plastic roses. Go figger. Anyway the reason I was paying attention was because my dad pronounces coyote like COY- oat. I tried to correct him but he would have none of it. He was too wrapped up in the story. Have you ever heard of such a bad pronunciation? Wile E. Coy – O – Tee and the roadrunner wouldn't even exist with my dad's way of saying coyote."

"Are you almost done with that scintillating story? Do you think that they have heard you yet?" Geez Zee. Zip it or no gig remember?"

"Well that's hardly fair, Lola. I am here aren't I. I came up with a great idea. I am just trying to pass the time. This is painfully boring if you just sit here and don't speak and just breathe."

"Keep your head and your voice down until I tell you it's scarin' time. Our timing has to be perfect, Lindsay, or this prank won't work. Got it?"

"I get it. I get it. Waiting is so hard though." Zee whines.

"Shhhhhhhh."

"Pick a headstone, any headstone, Addie, and put the blanket down in between the rows." Bernerd calls out. "I would suggest, however, that you pick one at the back, away from the road. Coyotes, if they are here, will probably come from that stand of trees, to the left."

I am having second thoughts, no wait, sixth thoughts about this adventure. I had no idea I would be this scared. I keep thinking that I hear snorting and snuffling. I keep getting glimpses of stuff out of the corner of my eye. It's probably only the skunk, just like Sigge says but oohboy. Do I have one elevated heart rate! Have you ever had that feeling that your eyeballs are throbbing with the beat of your heart? That's me, right now. My knees are locked into park. I am unable to move.

"Addie, really. Give me that blanket and follow me. I had no idea you would be such a jam tart." Sigge grabs the blanket and begins to march over the lumpy grass.

"Have a little more respect, Sigge, for the departed, please. You don't have to stomp about like a storm-trooper." suggests Bernerd as he hauls the wicker picnic basket out of the back of the hearse.

"I am just trying to get this experiment underway, Bernerd. We only have seven minutes until midnight. Come on, you guys. Shake a leg!"

I wait so that I can follow Bernerd. I don't want to be a trail-blazer in these circumstances. I just want to follow Sigge and Bernerd. They seem to know what they are doing and I don't feel so well. All of a sudden I have a splitting headache and I feel like I want to lie down. I feel like the energy is sapped from my body; like my brain is trying to escape my skull and that I am trapped in molasses. I have felt this before. It wasn't a good feeling then, and it is really un-good now. I can only describe it as impending doom.

"I don't know if you know this Sigge, but this is still a working cemetery. People are just dying to come here! Locals, who call this little burg home and who have homesteaded here for the past one hundred and fifty years, can still be buried here. Oh and for the record, that means that there may be some open, freshly dug grave sites. You will be able to tell if you see a mound of dirt about five feet high. Be careful and watch your step."

Bernerd chats about the history of St. Andrew's with such passion and excitement. He has done his homework and looks very comfortable here. It is as if he is conducting a tour in the middle of the day. I am trying to keep up and listen to what he is saying but I am lagging behind. I keep hearing things and my heart is racing. I don't want to be left behind but my legs don't want to bend.

"Hey Ladies. Let's try out the myth. Put the blanket down. Come on. Let's run around the church. Let's see if we disappear. I'll go first." Bernerd turns toward the church and the spire that is skewering the moon like an olive. He sprints toward the front doors of the church and stops.

"Sigge! What time is it?" Bernerd asks as he positions himself as if he is in sprinter's blocks.

"It is 11:59, brother dear, and counting." Sigge says. " Ten, nine, eight, …"

What if Bernerd does disappear? How will we explain his disappearance? Who will drive us home? Oh man, this is so creepy.

"ONE" Sigge yells and Bernerd bursts into action. He rounds the corner of the church and is completely out of sight.

Gone. Completely. Gone. Ohmigawd.

I notice a mound of dirt to the left of Sigge and Bernerd. I think it moves. I still have my phone on video and to distract myself from my jelly knees and pounding brain and suddenly invisible Bernerd I focus on the ground, the stars, the huge full moon. It is really horror-movie peaceful and heart throbbingly beautiful and if I could just relax it might even be fun. The church is to my right and its steeple is, of course, like in all scary movies and stories, silhouetted against the face of the neon melon moon.

The rustling and pounding of sneakers and the breathy almost soundless voice of Bernerd repeating

"Ohmigawd, Ohmigawd, Ohmigawd, Ohmigawd, Ohmigawd."

I see a flash of white skin, long red fingernails, and crazy smiling teeth. I see Sigge running toward me, I feel her grab the back of my sweater and tug me toward the hearse. I trip over my own feet, fall down and drop my phone. I scramble to find it. It is invisible in the dark. Sigge keeps running. I hear the hearse's motor attempt to start, then stop. I feel a very cool breeze against my cheek, and then a sudden calm scented with lavender. I should be screaming but I am not. My phone starts ringing. I see the light of its screen illuminate the leaves on the ground. It's to my left. I get to my knees, grab the phone and a handful of dirt and twigs. I push myself upright. I answer my phone. Sigge's face is hanging out the passenger side window, she is on the phone, yelling,

"ADDIE. HURRY. WE HAVE GOT TO GET OUT OF HERE NOW. OHMIGAWD."

I walk calmly and coolly to the door of the hearse. I slide into the back seat. I look back toward the cemetery. I see two red pinpoints of light in the darkness. I see the mist swirling, making mini-tornadoes, as if someone is moving through them. I imagine capes and long black dresses, top hats and canes; a very Victorian Gothic moment. I hear what I think is muffled laughter, throaty and evil. I roll up the window, and look in my hand. I see remnants of blue plastic roses. I start to shake. Bernerd finally guns the motor of the hearse, spits gravel into the air with the tires and leaves the lot in a cloud of dust, which swallows the fact that we were ever there.

"Now that was really scary and very interesting." whispers Sigge.

"That lavender thing, Lola, the laser pointers, complete freakin' genius!"

"Thanks Zee. We got 'em, hook, line and blue rose sinker."

19

The ride home is electric silence. You can almost hear our brains crackling. Bernerd's hands are gripping the steering wheel so tightly that you can see articulated knuckle bones through his skin. Rather appropriate for the moment but you can tell he is concentrating on getting us home safely. Bernerd takes a right turn on Pinewood to access our cul –de –sac. All is quiet and silent. Excellent. I look forward to the predictability of my room and my moon.

The hearse rolls up in front of my driveway. The front porch light is on. The house looks welcoming and warm. This is one of the nice changes that is happening since my mom has been trying to get better. Warmth, food, decorations, basic home stuff that's been missing but isn't any more it seems and I hope.

"I will call you two in the morning to debrief the evening." I say before I close the car door. "Let's get together and look at the video to see if we got any footage of the coyotes. Thanks you guys. Sorry I was so scared. Bye."

"Bye Addie. A demain".

I can hear faint strains of music playing in my house as I walk up the front steps. I hear Dean Martin is crooning Volare. My dad's favourite song. It must remind him of his favourite fabric, velour, eh! Hah. I kill myself.

Hey wait a minute. I am jarred out of my bad joke self as I notice that the screen door is ajar. No wonder I can hear music, the inside door is open too. This is weird. The creepy is continuing. This is not like my mom or dad. It's one thing to leave the door unlocked, it's completely another to leave the door open. Even at my mom's worst she never left the door open. My spidey senses are tingling. There is something odd here. Mom and dad are probably next door. There is no need to be nervous, Addie. Go in, read the note that they probably left for you, and relax.

When I step into the kitchen everything feels alright, except there is an over powering smell of onions or nasty body odour, sometimes it is hard to tell which is which. What I do know is that this is not the scent of my dad's usual cologne, Indulge. I put my phone down on the kitchen table and peel a blue plastic rose petal from my palm. Bernerd was not the only one clutching something to save their life. There is a really strange sound coming from the living room where the stereo is playing. It doesn't sound like the furnace or a blown speaker. It sounds like someone is trying to talk through a pillow. Ohmigawd. What if it is my mom and dad making out on the couch? Oh man. That would be embarrassing. Okay so here I go. I am going to cautiously and carefully peek into the living room and squint so I am not irreparably harmed by what I see if it is my parents.

"DAD! Ohmigawd. You are talking through a pillow. What happened? Did Mom do this to you. Did she snap or something?" I hear myself shrieking.

My dad is duct taped to his lazy boy chair with an indigo velvet decorative pillow taped over his mouth. The tape is florescent pink. His arms are taped to the arms of the chair, his legs are taped to the leg rest. His glass of beer is taped to his right hand, half full, his left is taped to the channel changer and then to the arm of the chair. The channel on the television is public broadcasting. Dad is watching Les Miserables live from Lincoln Centre with the volume off and Dean is still singing in the back ground. He is so totally taped to the chair that it is impossible for him to move anything but his eyelids.

I run to the kitchen to get scissors. I cut the tape that holds the pillow to his face first. Probably not my best idea but at least he can breathe.

"I am so glad to see you, Kiddo. I got home from work, sat down in my favorite chair, and the next thing I knew, I woke up because I couldn't move. You know how I get after work on the weekends, pooped. Well once I sit down, I am toast, warm and tasty."

"Where is Mom? Are you okay? Here let me cut the rest of this tape off of you."

"Your mom is at your Aunt Laura's. We were supposed to have dinner over there tonight. She is gonna wanna skin me for missing it. Well I guess there will be hell to pay tomorrow. There is no wrath like a woman scorned no matter how cute she is."

"Dad. You have spent the evening taped to a chair. How did this happen? Who did this to you? Are you okay?"

" I am fine except that I have to pee like a race horse. I have no idea who did this. I was asleep for Heaven's sake and you know that I sleep like a dead thing."

"I can't believe that you didn't wake up at all." I say to his back as he makes his way down the hall to the bathroom.

"Call your aunt please. Beg for my forgiveness. Tell both of them that I have been taped to a chair and couldn't lift even a finger for my beer to let them know that I had been detained. The beer thing will reassure them that for sure I am not kidding." The closing of the bathroom door punctuates his sentence.

As I dial my aunt's house on the landline, I can see a commotion out of the kitchen window. By commotion I mean: three police cars , flashing lights, and an ambulance all parked in front of the Baxter's house.

"What did your mother and your aunt say, Addie?" My dad asks as he ambles into the kitchen scratching and rubbing at the tape marks on his wrists.

"Nothing. I was distracted. I didn't call. Look!" I point out the window. "Let's get over there and find out what is going on. You also had better tell the police that our house was infiltrated and you were taped to your chair."

" Stay here until you call your mother. Tell her to stay at Laura's for the night. I don't like the look of this."

My dad jumps down the front stairs, runs around the circle, into the red and blue spinning lights of the Baxter's front yard. I've never seen him move like this ever. It would be impressive if it wasn't under such scary circumstances.

20

I leave all the lights on in the house. I leave my phone on the counter. I leave the door open. I run like a wild horse over to the Baxter's. Just as my mom is saying to me she would love to stay at Laura's because she was having such a nice time, I see a stretcher, with a body, being removed from the house into the waiting ambulance. I drop the phone receiver and bolt.

Sigge and Bernerd are standing at the end of their driveway watching as the stretcher is being loaded into the ambulance. Both of them are the color of sky blue sheets.

"Is he going to be okay? Is he going to be okay? Is he going to be okay?" Sigge is crying and Bernerd is hugging her.

"Of course he is, Sig. He's a tuffie!"

" I want to ride with him in the ambulance. I am going with him. I can't leave him alone. Ohmigawd Bern. I can't believe this has happened. I can't believe he would do this."

"Miss Baxter. If you are coming with us we need to leave now." The paramedic states very matter of factly, very directly.

"Go Sigge. I will be there as soon as I finish with the police. It's okay. Addie and her Dad are here. I will be okay. Don't worry about me, I am fine. Hold dad's hand, talk about our adventure. I will call mom and see you as soon as I can. It's okay, Sig. Go! Bye."

The ambulance pulls away from the house. It doesn't turn on its siren until it is out of the cul de sac. When the siren wails Bernerd asks my dad to come into the house with him. They talk, man to man. My dad is nodding and shaking his head. Bernerd must be explaining what he and Sigge walked in on. I am feeling useless on the driveway. I saunter up to one of the police officers and his police dog.

"What happened?" I ask the officer.

"Well Miss, this has been quite a wild night in your neighbour-hood. There seems to have been a break-in here, and a couple of other houses in the cul-de-sac had doors and windows rattled by someone or something. We aren't exactly sure what we are dealing with yet."

" It's usually so quiet, kinda, around here. That's a huge dog!" I am nervous. I feel responsible for all this for some inexplicable reason.

"What were you and your friends up to this evening?" Officer Wood scrutinizes my face.

"Not much. Just hangin'. You know. Teenager stuff. What's the dog's name?"

"Officer Rex."

"He's the King of Dogs is he?" I can be so lame sometimes.

"Well done. Not many people know what Rex means."

"You obviously haven't run into many kids who take English with Ms. Ostrowski at Silverwoods." I share and start to move toward the house.

"I would suggest that you do not go into the house, Miss. The crime scene guys are finished but it's probably better if you stay out here with me and Rex. It's not pretty."

"What do you mean it's not pretty?"

"I mean that there is a mess in there and well it's a mess and you shouldn't go in. 'nuff said."

Bernerd and my dad come back outside and stand beside me. My dad has his arm around Bernerd's shoulders and he seems to be holding Bernerd up.

"My scooter is gone. My Vespa, my favourite helmet. I shouldn't have left the keys on the kitchen counter. I should have had them with me. I worked so hard for that thing and now it's gone. Kaput. Vanished."

"Bernerd. It's okay, kid. It is only a thing. It will be found one way or another. You will have another one. Trust me." My dad is being very kind. Not that I don't think that he is kind, it just seems like he really cares and wants to help. "Things can be replaced. It's people that can't. Your dad will be fine. Let's get to the hospital. I am sorry to say that I don't drive Bernerd but I do make an excellent passenger. Here let me lie down in the back like a corpse and let's get to Emergency. Your dad will be happy to see you. It will make him feel much better to know you are there. Addie get in the passenger seat and let's go. Did you call your mother dear? I hope you didn't let her know what was going on. You never know how she is going to react to things. Let's go kids. Bernerd you will feel much better once you see your sister and your dad." And with that series of questions and statements, my dad lays down in the back of the hearse and drops immediately to sleep.

"Your dad is a really relaxed and solid guy, Addie. Thanks for coming over right away. It really helped. Sigge was going to go to pieces if she couldn't go with my dad."

"Did my dad tell you he spent the evening duct taped to his lounge chair? I got home and I heard some creepy noises and I crept into the living room and found him with a pillow taped to his face and the rest of him secured by crazy pink tape in his chair. He has no idea who did this as he was asleep at the time. The only reason he woke up is 'cause he couldn't move. This is very strange Bernerd. Why would someone target our sleepy little cul-de-sac? When I was talking to Officer Woods he said that other houses had their doors and windows rattled too! It wasn't just us. He also said the police have no idea who or WHAT did all of this. Bernerd? Do you think we are responsible for awakening some really evil spirits?"

"Addie, really. No. I don't think we rattled any evil spirits out of their ether. What would a spirit want with a Vespa and a helmet? What would a spirit want with pottery? Why would a spirit ransack our house, throw the contents of all our drawers on the floor, dump food from the fridge all over the kitchen and scribble with an oil pastel "You can run but you can't hide" on the walls of our living room? That kind of evil is from a human spirit. A mean-spirited, very sad, very tortured, very addled, human. There are many things I don't know about the spirit world Addie, but what I do know is that broken humans have broken spirits and they live among us, not anywhere else."

"Is that why you weren't scared at the cemetery tonight?" I ask.

" I was excited but not scared. The dead are dead. What can they do to you? I was unnerved by the skunk and the black clad creatures that emerged from behind the mound of grave dirt, and I was unnerved at the thought of being attacked by coyotes, but I wasn't scared of the dead. If I was I would not have bought the hearse!" Bernerd is very blunt. "But I am scared now. I am scared of losing my dad. I am scared of my mom being frightened and hurt. I am scared that another human could do this to my dad and my family. I am scared of how I feel right now. And Addie, all this fear has been caused by another human being, not a spirit."

"I wonder if this would have happened if we hadn't gone out tonight?" I consider.

"We didn't leave until quite late Addie. Whoever did this did this between 10:45 and whatever time it was when we got home, like maybe 12:30 at the latest. We left St. Andrew's at midnight and it takes forty-five minutes to get home so, we just missed whoever did this. You know, it occurs to me that your dad could have been in the process of being taped up while we were getting ready over here."

"Oh man, Bernerd, really? Now that is scary. Do you think we are being watched?" The horror of that thought hits me with a right hook.

"Quite possibly, Addie, we were. But not now I don't think. They got what they came for. Money from my dad's wallet, money from the cookie jar in the kitchen, money and a very rare and expensive baseball collector card from the secret stash in Sigge's room and a very small but valuable Emily Carr painting from our family room and worst of all my freakin' Vespa. Whoever did this knew what they were looking for and how to find stuff. Was anything taken from your house that you know of?"

"I have no idea, Bernerd. I wasn't there long enough to find out. I was only there long enough to unstick my dad from his chair and then run to your place. I guess we will find out when we get home if anything is missing."

"We are finally here. That was the longest and shortest drive of my life." sighs Bernerd.

"Stop the car at the Emergency door, Bern. You get out and go find your dad and Sigge. I will park the car for you. Don't worry. I won't crash it or anything . I've been taking lessons!" I need to lighten up this situation if I can. I feel so bad for the Baxters.

"Okay, Addie. Thanks. See you in a bit." Bernerd puts the car into park and throws himself out of the driver's side door. He sprints for the hospital doors.

I get out of the passenger side of the hearse and walk around to the driver's side. I take care as I put the car into drive. I encourage the car to be nice and let me drive it safely into a parking spot. My encouragement works. I pull away from the door and park in the nearest visitor parking spot. No muss, no fuss. I get out of the car and head for the waiting room to wait as this is what a waiting room is for.

21

My earbuds are in my ears, my eyes are closed, but my sense of touch is still intact. I know that the sliding door to the emergency room has opened. A slap of cool, crisp fall air hits my cheek. Mrs. Baxter has arrived. She is a woman on a mission.

"Hello. My name is Wanda Baxter. My husband Glen Baxter, was just admitted. Can you direct me to his room please?" Baxters are focussed and controlled.

"He's in room 832, Mrs. Baxter. Take the elevator down the hall to the eighth floor and his room is to your right when you get off." The admissions clerk tells her.

"Hi Mrs. B., Bernerd and Sigge are here too." I stand up and make my presence known.

"Hello Adelaide. I hope you don't mind that I don't stop and say a proper hello."

"Uh no. You have more important things to take care of. I don't

112

mind in the least. Bye!" I say as she swoops down the hallway to the elevator.

I sit back down to while away some time, maybe even sleep a little.

I feel the cool air of the open door again. This is a very busy place tonight. A parking lot security guard has approached the front desk. My eyes snap open when he starts to speak to the admissions lady.

"You have to believe me. I was doing my rounds of the lot, you know, like I usually do, every fifteen minutes, and on my first go round everything was just peachy. Quiet, dark, like it is this time of night. Then I see this hearse pull in. It parks in the visitor's spot. It is very clearly marked visitor. I look inside and see that there is a body laid out in the back of the hearse. I knock on the window a couple of times to make sure that it is not someone who has decided to use our lot for a nap. I really give a couple of good whomps on the window. No living person could live through the racket I was making so I figure that the funeral home has just made a pick-up from here and that they will clear out of the spot pretty soon. So I continue my walkabout. Fifteen minutes later I come back and the hearse is still there. So I go and look in the back window again and the body is gone. I am not seeing things, there was a body there fifteen minutes ago, and now there is not. I tell you, tonight has been one of the creepiest on record. You can tell it's a full moon. All the weirdoes are out and about."

The emergency room door opens again. My dad walks in wearing his navy blue velour track suit. He looks like he just woke up from a dead sleep. He is pale and his hair is not perfect. With his hands on his hips he scans the waiting area to see if he can see anyone he knows, like me, for instance.

"There you are Addie!" Dad says relieved to have found me. I was wondering where you wandered off to."

The security guard turns around, sees my dad, and predictably, faints.

"He must have a terrible flu." Dad says. "Or I am drop dead gorgeous. Hah! Don't get too close to him or me people. Now that's what I call an entrance."

"Hey Dad." I wave him over to my bank of seats. " Come and sit and wait with me. Mrs. Baxter just arrived. I don't think they need us to go up to the room. Let's just wait here."

A lot of hubbub occurs by the desk. A couple of orderlies have come to take care of the security guard and remove him from the room. It would hardly instill a sense of security if patients and their families see him lolling about on the floor. He is shuffled off behind a stainless steel door to be revived.

The phone rings at the nurse's desk. She nods and smiles as she answers it. When she puts down the receiver she calls me over to her station.

"Excuse me, dear, but is your name Addie?"

"It is."

"Your Baxter friends would like you to know that they will be here for the night and that you and your dad should go home and get some rest. They say thanks for the help and support and they will see you tomorrow. Alright?"

"Okay, thanks. Do you have a number for a cab? Could you give these car keys to the Baxters before they leave please?"

"There is a direct phone line right over there by the door. And I will make sure they get them. Thanks. Good night."

"C'mon dad. A taxi will be here in three minutes to take us home."

"But Addie I didn't even get to call you a cab."

"Go ahead, dad, do it now. I would hate to wreck your night."

"Yer a cab, Addie."

"Thanks for that Dad. Let's get home. It's been a long, sad night."

The cab enters the cul-de-sac and there is still a police car with its lights flashing parked in front of the Dixon's house.

"The Dixon's must have had something happen at their house tonight too, Dad. Let's go and see if they are all right. I won't be able to sleep until I know, okay?"

"I am not so sure that is such a good idea, Addie. Let me call Bob after the police leave. I will see if I can lend a hand then. Fortunately there is no ambulance there. What a frightening night, kiddo. I am so glad you are home safe and sound."

As dad and I enter our kitchen, the phone rings. Dean Martin is still singing and the television is still turned to PBS, though it has signed off to an off-season snow storm fluttering across the tv screen. My dad answers the phone while I attend to the entertainment electricals.

"Addie?" Dad yells from the kitchen. "Was Lindsay with you tonight? Have you seen her at all today?"

"Nope." I say. I want to add, like, as if... but I save that for another time. "Why?"

"Did you see her at school yesterday, by any chance?" Dad queries.

"Yep. I did. I saw her at 8:15 leaving the school with Lola. Why?" He's not answering my question and he is making me very nervous as he repeats what I say into the phone receiver.

"You are sure you saw her leaving school and not going into it?"

" Yes I am sure. What is wrong?" I ask my Dad.

"Just a sec, Bob, I will ask her. Addie, who did you say that Lindsay left with yesterday?"

" I think I saw her leave with Lola Lambert."

"This is very important Addie. Did she or did she not leave with Lola Lambert?" My dad is very serious, not a shred of humour anywhere in his voice.

"I am positive. She left with Lola. Can you tell me why?"

My dad shushes me with a wave of his hand.

"What street do the Lamberts live on Addie? Bob can't seem to find their phone number on line. He is losing his mind. Do you happen to know?"

"Their phone number is unlisted because Lola's dad is a rock star! I have it in my phone. Here, it's 778-912-8812. Hope that helps."

"Bob, the number is 778-912-8812. Let me know what you find out. It doesn't matter what time it is. Lindsay is like my own daughter. Let me know when you find her. It's okay Bob. It will be okay. She's fine I am sure. Get back to me. I will be waiting." Dad shakes his head as he hangs up the phone.

"I am sure glad I don't have to worry about you like they have to worry about that Lindsay. You have a good head on your shoulders Addie. Thanks for that. Oh and to answer your question, Lindsay hasn't been home since before school yesterday. The police are asking questions. They think Lindsay may be involved in the shenanigans that went on in the cul de sac this evening."

"Dad . I think I should make some coffee. I don't think we'll be sleeping tonight."

"You might be right my little ginger kitty. It's 3:30 already. Time flies when your stuck in a crime scene! Hah! Did you hear that Addie! Stuck in a crime scene. Gawd. I kill myself."

Good grief. How can he joke at a time like this? Lindsay is missing and he was taped to a chair. Omigawd. This is one huge true nightmare. I need my room.

"Dad? Are you okay? Do you mind if I go and hang in my room for a bit or do you need the company?"

"Go ahead, Addie. I'll find some dreary old movie to watch on TV and nap in my chair. I want to wait for Bob to call back. Go relax if you can. I am perfectly perfect. Except for the Lindsay thing, of course."

"Thanks, Dad."

I drag myself up the stairs from the kitchen to my room.

Wait a minute. That's weird. I don't leave my bedroom door open, ever. My door is open and I can see that every one of my dresser drawers is dumped on the floor. Written on the wall above my bed in ruby red lipstick is "You say party I say, thanks Sucka!"

"DAAAAAAAAAAAAAAAAAAA AAAAAAAAAAAAAAAAAAAAAA AAD!"

I slam the door to my room and jump down the stairs into the kitchen. I am breathing hard and fast. I am shaking in my slippers.

"What is it Addie? What is wrong?" Dad springs to action out of his chair and onto the black and white checkerboard of the kitchen floor. I have not seen him move so fast, or so often as I have in the past couple of hours.

"Come, come and see this! The sanctity of my room has been vandalized. Omigawd, I feel so violated!"

Both of us take the stairs to my room two at a time.

" Whoa! What do we have here besides a giant mess?" My dad steps into my room and checks out the contents of my closet."

"Currently boogie-man free!" he says, composed and calm and very in control.

"We better look around and make sure that there is nothing stolen or any more words of wisdom written on our walls.

Does this statement make sense to you Addie? Does it mean anything? Does this sound or look like something Lindsay would write to you?"

My dad is clearly concerned and worried. He drapes his navy blue velour arm around my shoulders. He pulls me in tight, like he won't ever let me out of his sight. Like he is thankful to be at home with me, and that he is glad that I am safe and warm and secure.

"It doesn't sound like a Lindsay thing at all. Plus she likes my room, or at least she used to. I don't think she would do anything like this. I can't imagine who could have…." *There is something kinda familiar about this message but then kinda not.*

"What about the Lola person? Would she do something like this?" Dad is clearly puzzled.

" I don't think so Dad. None of this makes any sense. My friends aren't violent vandals. Besides wanting my part in the play, Lola would have no reason to do any of this I don't think. If she is the kind of person that would do this just to be in a play, well, she can have the part. Good Grief. Plus what could Lindsay gain by hurting Mr. Baxter? It is so not her character. All of this is so confusing."

The phone rings in the kitchen. My dad leaps into the hallway and jumps down the stairs. My heart leaps into my throat. He gets to the phone before it rings a second time. I peek my head into the hallway to eavesdrop on his conversation.

"Bob? Thank goodness you tracked her down. Where was she? Oh, I see. Is she at home now? Is she all right? Great. Is there anything Addie or I can do? Well all right. We will. Thanks. We will see you in the morning." My dad's shoulders visibly relax as he hangs up the phone. They are no longer hugging his ears. "Lindsay is home and all in one piece. She was at Lola's. Thanks for the number, Addie."

"Excellent news, dad . No probs. Now let's both try and get some sleep."

Dad yawns.

"I am going to sleep on the floor in your room if you don't mind, dad. That nasty stench of onions and the bad graffiti on my wall have me a little wigged out."

"No problem, sweetie. I will go and open the window in your lair now, then clean up that scribble once I get up."

"Thanks dad. Thanks for everything tonight. You make everything so much better, weirder but definitely better."

22

I am curled up squirrel-like in a nest that I have created at the foot of my parents' bed. I used to sleep here, like this, when I was little and I had bad dreams. I was always safe here, protected, and the bad dreams would always dissipate in the morning. But that's the difference between being little and now. Bad dreams linger and become the mood of my day. My dad is up and bustling about. He is moving between my room and the kitchen. I can see him through the semi-closed door of his room and my sticky morning eyes. I can smell pine-fresh cleaner and burnt toast. I better get up.

It is a sunny, clear day. You can tell it is fall by the way the light reflects off of the street and houses through the white gauzy curtains of my parents' room. The sun casts a soft golden sheen over the sky, not all harsh angles like the summer. The sky itself is a pale baby blue and the scent of smoke is faint but present in the air. Coffee is pulling me to the kitchen on a long witchy finger of its aroma. I have to get up. Sigge and Bernerd are going to need me.

I brush my teeth, wash last night off of my face, and descend the stairs into the kitchen.

"Addie, petunia, good morning sweetie. You will be surprised at how late you did not sleep!" my dad smiles and hands me my favourite Peter Rabbit mug filled with coffee.

" Thanks for this. What time is it?" I ask, taking a loud slurp.

"Nine." Dad says.

"Whoa! That's weird. You are up really early. Are you okay?"

" I am fine, Addie. The police will be here soon, though. I wanted them to see the writing on the wall of your room. I took a polaroid of it and then thought they might need to see it before I wash the wall. I don't want them to think that I was destroying evidence or anything. I also kept the duct tape. Who knows, there might be some finger prints on it that they can identify. Do you know if Lindsay or Lola are whizzes with duct tape?"

"Nah. I don't think so. Lindsay wasn't much good with knots in Brownies and I can't imagine her learning confinement tactics in Home Ec. I don't know Lola very well, but I somehow doubt her skills with tape too. They are just regular high school girls dad. They don't assault people or ransack neighbourhoods. They'd mess their hair!"

"I hope that is the case, Addie. I truly do. Oh, by the way, where were you and Sigge and Bernerd last night?" Dad throws that grenade of a question into the conversation and for some reason I feel like I have done something wrong, that I have done something to feel guilty about.

"Well, we were on an adventure. We went out to the old church at St. Andrew's. We were doing some investigative reporting on a pack of wild coyotes and local folklore."

"Did you run around the church, counter-clockwise, three times, under the full moon, as the clock struck midnight?" Dad asks with a silly smirk on his face.

"Bernerd almost did but something emerged from an open grave and chased us away! Really. It was so scary and creepy. I thought for sure Bernerd was going to disappear. The entities from the deep did him a favour I think." My heart is pounding as I tell Dad about the adventure.

"Aw, he would have been fine. Bernerd has a kind heart and a good soul. He wouldn't have disappeared unless he wanted to. I did that run, you know, back in the day. I ran around the church on a dare. I didn't disappear, as you can clearly see, and I am just fine. Teenage right of passage. I get it Addie. And considering the hijinx that went on around here last night, you are lucky to have been there and not here! I don't like to think about what might have happened if you kids had all been around here last night. OOOBoy. That's a scary thought."

"Have you told Mom about what happened last night, yet?" I ask.

"No Addie I have not. She said she is having a good visit with Laura and that she is going to stay with her for a couple more days."

"That's convenient and odd don't you think?" I say.

"Convenient yes, odd no. Laura is on holidays and you know how close she and your mother are. They never get to spend enough time together. It's something Dee needs don't you think?" Dad is relieved. I can hear it in his voice. One less person to worry about.

"Sure. I guess." I too am relieved.

I look out of the kitchen window at the calm that seems to have descended on our cul de sac. It is the usual Sunday morning activities of lawn mowers cleaning up yards for the last time before the snow flies. Little kids are riding their bikes in circles around the cul de sac, oblivious to their own impending teenage trials, squealing with delight and their immediate freedom. There are faces of mothers in windows watching their little darlings conquer two-wheeler fear, there are dads raking leaves and washing cars, there are teenagers languishing on their front doorsteps with their first cup of coffee of the day relishing the last few rays of warmth from the sun before the big chill sets in for the next nine months. I know it is not silent out there, but it seems like it is from in here. Perfect and silent and contained in a bell jar, so the last thing I need is my mom to make Lindsay and Bob and Dot's life even more unpleasant and loud, right now. When my mom is good, she is very, very good, but when she is bad, well she can be a freakin' nightmare. I am glad she is not here.

As this thought tickles my brain, a police cruiser pulls up in front of our house re-applying the smeared lipstick of last night's bad memory.

"DAAAAAD!" I yell . "The police are here."

I take a seat at the kitchen table as my dad lets two policemen in. There is Officer Woods with the dog Officer Rex, from last night, and another giant navy blue man with a camera. I am glad that they are here. They bring a kind of closure to the nastiness but they also point up the seriousness of it all. If this stuff didn't matter we would just be a case number. My little world has definitely changed.

Dad takes the police up to my room to show them the scrawl on my wall and the man-made mess in my room. When they all return to the kitchen Dad hands them a clear plastic bag filled with the pink duct tape that I cut off of him.

"So officers, if weren't for the quick thinking action of my daughter Addie here, I may still be taped to my chair! Total whiz with scissors."

The officers nod and almost smile. My dad looks really wirey skinny compared to these guys. The contrast is interesting; q-tip versus hair brush.

"With your permission Mr. Sinclair, we need to take Addie's fingerprints. Did you wear gloves when you were removing the tape from your dad, Miss?" Officer Woods asks.

"Uh, no. I just wanted to get my dad unstuck as quickly as possible and have him be able to breathe. Leaving my fingerprints behind was the last thing on my mind. Take my fingerprints, please. I had nothing to do with any of this. Oh. How is Rex?"

"He's just fine, Miss Addie, thank-you. He is in the car. Now let's get these fingerprints dealt with."

23

The police pack up and head out. They leave the cul de sac as they found it this morning. Quiet and in order. My dad fills a red plastic bucket with a fruit scented cleaner to wash the lipstick off of my walls. I wash my hands to get the black ink out from underneath my fingernails. It has been an eventful morning and it is still only 10:30 am. It is a respectable time to visit the Baxters , I think. I need to see if they are okay.

"Dad, I am off to see the Baxters, okay? I will come home for lunch. Can you take me and Bernerd and Sigge to Juniors for burgers?" I am shouting as I leave the house so he can hear me.

A muffled, "We'll see" wafts down from my room on the scent of oranges and green apples. "Talk to me when you get home."

"Okay, see ya later." The screen door closes and latches behind me.

I stand at the top of our porch landing and survey my neighbourhood. It's hard to believe that less than six hours ago multiple police cars and their spinning lights were trying to make sense of the mayhem that had ensued in our world. Not one house in the cul de sac escaped some form of terror. The Macgregors had their pumpkin patch completely destroyed, the Valeurs found their mailbox beheaded from its post, the Rodriguez's had scratches all down the side of their brand new mini-van. Senseless, nasty behaviour. Who could have done this and why choose this neighbourhood? It seems so random and creepy. Weird that it all happened last night too, when all the big kids were out and about. Oh well. The police are on it. I am sure they will solve this.

I saunter to Sigge's, appreciating the sun and the quiet. The lime green of Bernerd's hearse is a beautiful contrast to the navy blue exterior of their house. Their drapes are open, the windows are open, and a vacuum is whirring in the living room. A John Phillip Sousa March is spilling into the front yard. The nasty spirits that took over the Baxter's house last night are being driven out by the sound of brass and military precision cleaning. I would expect nothing less.

No one hears my knock on the front door. I try the handle. It is locked. I try it again and an alarm goes off. A siren starts blaring and every window around the cul de sac has a nose plastered to a window. I turn around and shrug my shoulders and wave to let everyone know it's just me Addie Sinclair, causing another ruckus yet again. Good Grief. I back away and gingerly step down the stairs. I wait for someone to open the door.

There is the sound of someone fumbling to open a multitude of locks and the music quickly snaps off. Someone is moving room to room closing windows and draperies as they go. It is suddenly quiet and dark and ominous.

This is not what I would expect.

Mrs. Baxter opens the door just enough to see who it is. When she realizes it's only me, she opens the door, takes me by the elbow and pulls me into the house. The overwhelming scent of pine cleaner reminds me of elementary school and vomit. The atmosphere of their house changed within seconds from a home to a fortress. I am scared. This is so un-Baxter. Mrs. B closes the door behind me and turns five locks. Sigge and Bernerd are at the top of the stairs looking down at the foyer to see who their mom has let in.

"Oh Addie. We are not quite used to the alarm just yet! Sorry. You know, we had that thing installed when we first moved in here last March, but we never used it."

"I am really sorry I tried to open the door. It's just that I thought it was stuck and well it's usually always open and....Sorry. I should know better." Everyone is looking at me with huge wide eyes. "Gee, if this is a bad time, I'll go and maybe come back later."

"Addie it's okay. We are all a little shaken up. That siren stirred up the fear all over again." Mrs. Baxter gives me a hug. Sigge and Bernerd descend the stairs. The two of them don't look so good.

"Let's all go into the kitchen. We can sit and have tea and cookies and chat." Mrs. Baxter shepherds the three of us down the hall. Her kids are looking rather zombie like and I am nervous because something is really wrong here.

Sigge and Bernerd both sit on the same side of the table. Their chairs are touching and they seem like they don't want to be too far from one another. Neither one of them has said a word.

I am very uncomfortable . Maybe if I do something we will all feel better.

"Here Mrs. Baxter. Let me help you with those cups, and you sit. I will take care of you guys. I am fine. You are not. How is Mr. Baxter this morning?" I want this to be light-hearted and not sad. The Baxters are my strength I don't want them to be unhappy.

'Well, Addie, good news and bad news. The good news is that Mr. B is alive. The bad news is that the bonk on the head was more serious than first suspected. Mr. Baxter takes a blood thinning medication and the last thing he needed was a blow to the head. The doctors are trying to keep him stable and comfortable. That's what we know right now. Visiting hours start at 11:00 so I will be toddling over there shortly. Was everything okay at your house when you got home from the adventure?

"Except for the fact that my dad was duct taped to his lounge chair, and that someone ransacked my room and wrote on my wall in lipstick, everything was fine. It is so scary, Mrs. B. I understand why you activated your alarm. If we had an alarm I would have had it ready to go too. As it was I slept on the floor in my parents' room last night. I would never have gotten to sleep without the sound of my dad's snoring. Oddly enough it is very comforting." I share.

"The cemetery was a piece of cake compared to coming back in here this morning. My mom and I stayed at the hospital and Bernerd came home, called a 24 hour emergency locksmith and read the operating manual for the alarm system. That's why he looks like he does." Sigge smiled a sympathetic smile in the direction of her brother.

"Adrenalin and caffeine are the fluids du jour." Bernerd says without a twinkle.

Mrs. Baxter places the teapot on the counter. She pours boiling water from the kettle into the teapot until it covers the dangling silver tea ball in the center of the pot.

"That should do it." Mrs. Baxter announces. " Set the oven timer for five minutes and let it steep kids. Then I will break out the cookies."

That was the closest thing to happy that I had seen in this kitchen in ten whole minutes. We all sit and stare at the center of the table. Words are unavailable today.

The timer beeps and I get up to claim the teapot and its subsequent pouring rights. On the counter by the phone is a photograph of someone who looks familiar.

"Hey." I say, as I pick it up and look really closely at the face. "That's a really nice picture of Kevin".

"Kevin? That's not a Kevin. That's Eric." explains Bernerd. "Our brother. We had to give that "nice" photo to the police so they would know who they are looking for. Nice. Hardly a word that I would use to describe that jerk."

The jangle of the phone startles all of us. I drop the photo on the floor. Mrs. Baxter answers it and is nodding and saying a series of yesses and okays. She hangs up and announces,

"Bern, you are in luck. The police have found your Vespa and your helmet. That's the good news. The bad news is where they found it."

"Don't tell me, let me guess, Mom." Bernerd sneers.

"They found my scooter at that effin' lowlife's flop house, right?"

"Bernerd, Eric is your brother. And yes dear, that is exactly where they found it. His last known address."

I can see a transformation taking hold of Sigge. She is pale and trembling. She is emitting a high pitched sound that only me and dogs can hear.

"Ohmigawdohmigawdohmigawd. How did he find us? How did he find us, Mom?"

Sigge is rocking back and forth in her chair, hugging her knees, hiding her face, softly weeping. Every once in a while the word noooooooo, breaks her sobs in two and Bernerd and her mom take turns patting her back.

"I don't know, sweetheart. We have been so careful. I just don't know how this could happen. I just don't know why he would do this. He's broken Sigge. That's what it is. He is just broken."

I am completely breathless. I have to go home. My brain is pounding. There is nothing more I can do. I have to leave. I can't believe what I have done.

I am numb all over. The same fear that held me in its clammy hands last night has a really firm grip on my heart and my throat. I have got to get out of here. I have got to get the hell out of this kitchen. I forget about hanging around having tea and cookies. I step on the face of "Kevin" as I run to the hallway to make my escape out of the front door. I can't even bring myself to say good-bye. It hurts too much.

I know how Eric found them. I know how Eric found them. I know how Eric found them.

Ohmigawd.

I know how Eric found them.

I so know.

24

Running home from Sigge's this time, right now, is different than it has ever been. I am running away from her and her family with a heavy guilty knot for a heart. I am running home to hide in my room and talk to the moon. I need to make sense of this. I can't let them know it was me. That all of this terror and horror and pain is all my fault. They will hate me forever.

I am completely winded when I get to my door. I can see my dad through the screen door sitting at the kitchen table reading the newspaper and relaxing. I have been gone only twenty minutes but it feels like forever.

I am thankful he is here and not in the hospital. I am thankful for his weirdness. I am thankful he wasn't hurt last night. I can't believe that answering Sigge's phone a week ago could have caused all of this destruction.

"Hey!" I say.

"That was quick," he says rather distractedly, " Is everything okay over there?"

"The Baxter's house feels really weird and creepy this morning. I had to come home. Something just doesn't feel quite right. I need to hang around with you today I think."

"You must be more shaken than stirred!" jokes my dad.

I roll my eyes.

"Our little cul de sac made the paper this morning!" Dad reveals. " The thundering horde of vandals that shook us all to the core as well as the attack on Mr. Baxter are major front page news stories."

Ohmigawd. I should hang a really old cell phone around my neck as a reminder of my stupidity. I did this. It was Eric AND ME that wreaked havoc in our little haven. If only I had not answered the stupid phone, had I not been sucked in by his honey voice.

"I guess our attempt to keep this from Mom will be thwarted." I say.

"If we are lucky Auntie Laura won't take the paper and all of our worry will be a moot point. Anyhoo, why don't we decide where we are going to go for dinner. I will spring for something delicious so we don't have to clean up again today. What do you say?" Dad is all smiles.

"I say, please can we go to the CRAB BUCKET? It's been my favourite for years and we haven't gone there since the last time that we went with the Dixon's. Wait. Omigawd. I have an idea. Why don't we call the Dixons and all of us can go, together. It might be a nice way to end this weekend and they may want to get out of the house so they don't have to look at one another any more. I am sure Lindsay will want to go out and hang with someone other than Bob and Dot. You know how wound up Dot can get! I bet the silence around there is deafening and that Lindsay is domestic slave-girl. I am sure whatever is going on over there is not very pleasant. Plus you need a distraction from our invaded space and I need to re-kindle an old friendship. C'mon Dad. Burn up the phone lines!" I am breathless in my excitement.

"Addie that is a great idea. I will call Bob and Dot and see if they are game. But don't hold your breath now, darling". They may not want to socialize."

"I know, Dad, but Danger Mom is not here and the Dixons are as much social pariahs as we are. Lindsay is a suspected felon now, so her parents have no reason to be so high and mighty. Don't get me wrong, Dad. I love the Dixon's but you know. Things get kinda weird when friendships end for the wrong reasons."

"Tru dat." Dad mutters.

"What did you say? You aren't trying to be hip or anything are you dad?"

"Don't need to try darlin'. I already am." Dad smiles and picks up the phone. "Who knew it could feel so good to make a phone call, Addie! Hope it all pans out."

"I am going to take a nap, dad, okay?" Wake me up before you go, go…."

"WHAM, right back at cha." Dad winks and slams his hand on the kitchen counter as I make my way up the stairs to my room again. I hear him say into the receiver:

"Hey Bob! Listen, Addie and I had a great idea for dinner tonight. What do you think about us......"

I will get the results of the survey later. But first, the moon.

Finally sanctuary. The ripe peachy fruity apple lemon smell of the cleaner my dad used to wash my wall has freshened the air of my room. He has left the window open wide to let the bad spirits out and to refresh mine. There is a faint smudge of pink on my wall which reminds me of the scrawl but it will fade with time or, perhaps I will scrawl my own inspirational saying there on the wall and even bejewel it. I wrap myself up in bed with my zebra fuzzy blanket and lie down on my side on my bed, to put the smudge behind me. I stare out of the window. The cool breeze and the calm of mid-day are just what my heavy heart needs. That and a heart to heart with my only constant, distant friend.

"So Moon, here I am again, muddled and frightened about my next move. I have hurt the Baxters irreparably as you probably witnessed. They have been my best friends and look what my behaviour has done. There is only one thing for me to do now isn't there? And it is so not going to be easy. They have become my life and my besties, Sigge and Bernerd. But I am not good for them. I am not good for their family. It's time to say good-bye. It's going to be hard but it has to be done. For their sakes, definitely, not mine. So what do you think? Ah, I understand your silence. You are thinking about this one. You are wondering about the wisdom of this. You are wondering how I can abandon them and not tell them the truth. I can see you faintly in the distance. You seem to be fading away from me. You seem to want to leave this conversation. Are you abandoning me? Especially at a time when I really, really, really, need you? Really? Okay. Fine. I will do this on my own. It's not as if you are offering me much in the way of constructive advice anyway. Thanks Moon. Enjoy the night, jerk."

If I am going to do this, I really need some sleep.

25

Mornings stay darker longer now. The clocks are on the verge of falling backwards. Halloween is this weekend and there is a crispness in the air. Brittle brown and gold oak leaves crunch under my feet as I walk toward the school. It is seven o'clock and Mr. Moore, the janitor, will be unlocking the school doors right about now. The place will be almost deserted. There will be one or two teachers decompressing in their classrooms, making coffee, entering marks without any whining, by students anyway, and shiny start of the week floors will welcome me.

I have to be quick about this. I told Lindsay last night at dinner that I would meet her at the corner at eight so that we could walk to school together. I want to leave early so I don't bump into Sigge or Bernerd.

The drama room is at the back of the school by the park. The posting for Lucy will be on the door of the Drama room if Mr. Noble is a man of his word and name. The closer I get to the room, breathing becomes difficult. I am gulping air like it's a last meal. What has gotten into my resolve? From down the hall I can see the bright acid yellow call back list posted on the door. My heart thumps audibly through my jacket. I slow down my steps. I have to believe that I am doing the right thing. I am doing the right thing.

I take a black felt pen out of my jacket pocket. I look at the list.

— FINAL CAST LIST FOR DRACULA —

Bernerd Baxter – DRACULA

Addie Sinclair – LUCY

Bennet Black – RENFIELD

I only read so far before I start to tear up. My eyes are not cooperating with my brain.

I am doing the right thing. I am doing the right thing. I am doing the right thing.

I take the cap off of the felt pen and very slowly, very deliberately, I draw a giant **X** through my name. I insert Lola Lambert's name beside the giant *X*. Lola is now Lucy.

I am doing the right thing. I am doing the right thing. I think I am doing the right thing.

Good. It's done and there is still enough time to get home, get organized, and meet Lindsay at the corner. Lola is now Lucy. That has a nice ring to it now doesn't it?

Ohmigawd.

What have I done?

I've got to get home. A brisk jog is in order.

As I approach the front door of my house, I see Lindsay sitting on the front step. She is the Lindsay of yore. No leather, no eyeliner, no beach hair. No Zee in sight.

"Hey, where were you?" Lindsay asks. " I was waiting here until you came out."

"Oh I went for a run. I have so much stuff running through my head. Got to pound it out through my feet." I say and hope she believes me. I walk up the stairs to the door.

"It feels good to sit here again. It's been a long time." Lindsay sighs. "Sorry, as a word, just doesn't seem like enough to say, Addie."

"Oh now Linds, don't go quoting bad song lyrics. I hear ya. Parents are weird. They only want the best for us but sometimes they don't know what they are doing." I want to make her feel better. I want to make me feel better. "Do you want a cup of coffee while you wait? Do you want to come in or sit on the steps? I will just be a couple of minutes. Gotta get the back pack in order, you know, morning stuff."

"Nah. I 'll just wait out here and watch the sun come up.It is so peaceful right this second it's hard to believe what a crazy weekend it was around here."

"I'll be two seconds." The screen door closes behind me. There is something so comfortable about having Lindsay sit on the step. She always used to wait for me out there. Even in the winter she would sit on the step and breathe out giant clouds to pass the time. Right now she has a pile of books on her lap, red sneakers on her feet, blue jeans and a white hoodie on her self. It looks like she belongs here, that she never left me behind. By sitting on the step Lindsay is telling me she is my friend again. That my house is safe and that she needs me once more. Friendship can be so elastic.

I bound up the stairs to my room. My phone is ringing. I pick it up and read the call display. Signe Baxter. I ignore the call. It stops ringing for my attention. I take the necessary steps to block that number. Necessary steps. To keep her safe. To keep him safe. I leave my phone at home, to keep us all safe.

Back down the stairs, backpack on back, through the kitchen, out the door, lock the door, and

"C'mon Linds, Let's go!"

The two of us jump down the front steps and race to the stop sign at the end of the cul de sac.

"Just like when we were little isn't it Lindsay. I will win tomorrow!"

As we are catching our breath, Lindsay looks at her feet and starts to kick whatever is on the sidewalk in front of her over the curb: twigs, pebbles and crunchy leaves.

"Listen Addie. Lola and I had absolutely nothing to do with hurting Mr. Baxter or breaking into your house or any of that. Really. I know I told you this last night at dinner, but really, you have to believe me."

"Fine. I believe you, but I don't think it's me that you have to convince. I think it is the police that might need convincing. If it wasn't you guys, who do you think did it?"

"How the hell should I know, Addie. It is not as if I hang around criminals, unless you count yourself..."

"Hey, Wait a minute. It was just a question. Do you really hate me that much? Do you really believe that I am a criminal? Because if you do Lindsay, wow. You are not who I thought you were."

"Oh man. I am so scared , Addie. No I do not hate you and it seems no matter what I say it gets me into trouble. I really need a friend right now, and you know me better than anyone. You know I couldn't do anything like they say we did."

"I do know Lindsay. I told my dad that yesterday."

"Plus I can prove that I was nowhere near this place on Saturday night."

"You have an alibi?" I ask.

"Gawd. You make me sound so dangerous. Yes I do have an alibi, if you want to call it that. Ewwww. I feel so dirty and guilty." Lindsay flips up the hood of her hoodie and pulls the zipper right up underneath her chin.

"Okay, spill it. Where were you? Were you at a bar with Lola? Do you have a fake ID? Is that why you are so scared? Is that why you are so afraid of the police?" I am intrigued.

"Addie. I am afraid because I am under suspicion of assault with intent. And no I wasn't at a bar. Geez."

"Okay. So where were you?" I am getting impatient.

"I, um, we were out at St. Andrew's."

"WTF Lindsay. No freakin' way. I don't believe you."

"I can prove it, Addie. Really. I almost peed my pants when the skunk came out of the shrubs and the blue plastic rose petals were a nice touch, don't you think? I am also a whiz with laser pointers. Does any of this sound familiar?"

"I was so scared." I whisper. I can feel the fear all over again for a split second, and then I burst.

"You are a complete jerk, Lindsay! I was so scared and you almost gave us all heart attacks. No wonder the cackling sounded familiar and creepy. It was you."

"Comedic gold, right? You guys were hilarious. Whoa. Hold everything, Addie. I just had a thought. Me and Lola are kind of like heroes. If we hadn't scared the living daylights out of you guys you wouldn't have gotten home in time to find Mr. Baxter or your dad. We kind of did you a favour."

"Nice favour. How are you gonna prove you were there?" I ask.

"That's where you and the Baxter's come in. You are going to exonerate Lola and me. You guys are going to provide us with our alibi."

"I should have known you had a motive other than being my friend, Lindsay." I snarl. "How do you expect us to help?"

"Think back to Saturday night. What did you have in your hand, Addie?"

"My phone. On camera! Ah I get it. Maybe we have you on film. That would be perfect!"

"Exactly. Now can you call Sigge?" Lindsay asks.

"No can do, Lindseroo. It's all up to you!" I Seuss it up to lighten my mood. "See ya later. Do we have geo today?"

" Yup. I will save you a seat." Linsday offers.

"Okay. Bye. Let me know how the call to Sigge works out. My phone is at home. I will check the photos later." This Lindsay moment feels both weird and normal, oxymoronic in fact. I am glad I have a project for later, to keep my brain occupied, to keep the guilt at bay.

26

Lindsay has saved me a seat in front of her in geo class. There is no Lola so far, and no Sigge. I wonder if Lola knows about the switch. I wonder if Mr. Noble knows about the switch. I wonder if Bernerd…

Before I can finish that thought, Lola enters. She is all boots and black leather. She has a million tiny braids in her hair and her eyes are glittering silver. She is wearing blood red lipstick and ultra pale make-up. She looks untouchable and untortured. She marches across the front of the classroom and deposits her late slip onto Ms. Clayton's desk. She scans the room to see if I am here. She finds me and winks. Lola knows.

"Sorry to interrupt, Ms. Clayton, but Sinclair there, is wanted in the counselling office. Ms. Plunkett needs to see her." Lola is pointing a sculptured, claw-like fingernail in my direction.

"That's fine and that's all Lola. Take a seat, please." Ms. Clayton gives me a sympathetic look. "Addie, off you go.

Take your things with you."

There has obviously been some communication between Ms. Plunkett and Ms. Clayton prior to this moment. Ms. Clayton wouldn't tell me to take my books and stuff if she expected me to return, shortly. I have been shivering most of the day but it has now become full blown shaking. I am nerves and fear and guilt. I pick up my binder and look at Lindsay for some moral support. Nothing, nada. Just a blank, flat, vacant stare. I have an auditory hallucination of an elastic snapping. The silent snap spurs my feet into action.

I walk out of the room and Ms. Clayton follows me.

"Whatever it is Addie, it will all work out. Things always do. You'll see. Don't worry. You will be just fine."

"Thanks, Ms. C.. I apologize for interrupting your class. That's two in a row. Maybe you'll get some teaching done when I am not in the room. Thanks for the nice words. I appreciate them, really." I head toward the counselling office and wonder what's up now.

For the first time ever the counselling department is empty and quiet. The only open door is Ms. Plunkett's. I can hear music softly playing in her office. I shuffle my feet over to her door and knock really quietly.

"Hi. Ms. Plunkett? You wanted to see me?" I say with a quiver.

"Oh Addie. C'mon in and sit. I'll shut the door." Ms. Plunkett smiles her all knowing smile and pushes the door so it latches. "Are you feeling alright dear? You are looking a little pale."

"I am just kind of curious about why I am here that's all." I am looking at the floor, at my shoes, at the posters on the wall and finally Ms. Plunkett's face. She looks concerned.

"Well, there are a couple of reasons actually. I have just heard from the Baxters about what occurred on the weekend. Sigge has been trying to reach you but has not been successful. She and her mom want you to know that Sigge is going to be away from school for a while. She wants to stay at home until her dad's condition improves and that their family issues get resolved. She is having a tough time right now and she wanted you to know. Sigge really needs a friend during this time Addie. I hope you can lend her some moral support. She has been very good to you."

"What about Bernerd? Is he going to be staying home too?" I ask a little too enthusiastically. *I hope he is so that Dracula will be cancelled.*

"No Addie. Bernerd will be here. It is his final year of high school and he feels this is where he should be. Plus he made a commitment to Mr. Noble to play Dracula and to quote Bernerd "Dracula, I will be." Which brings me to my other reason for having you come down to my office. Mr. Noble dropped by this morning with this."

Damn.

Ms. Plunkett is holding the cast list in her hand. My X and Lola's name are huge and obvious.

"Is there anything you want to tell me about this, Addie? I was under the impression that you really wanted to play the part of Lucy. Why did you change your mind?"

"It's for the best Ms. Plunkett, really. Lola will be an excellent Lucy and no one will have to worry about me doing something stupid and messing everything up. You know how I can be."

"Addie it is only a play. There is nothing you could do to mess it up."

"Trust me. It will be better for Sigge and Bernerd and me and Lola. Nuff said. Can I go now?"

"One last thing, Addie. Is everything okay at home? Is your mom alright?"

"Look, Ms. Plunkett. Why does it always come back to my mom? Not being Lucy is my choice. Home is fine. My mom is fine. My dad is ridiculous, and this weekend is Halloween. I couldn't be happier. So, thank-you for your concern but I would like to go home now."

"That's fine Addie. Just remember to contact Sigge. She needs to talk to you."

"I don't think so, Ms. P.. It's better if I don't. Thanks."

I stand up to leave and a wave of nausea swells up over me. I run out of Ms. Plunkett's office and out of the front door of the school. I vomit right outside the doors. I wipe my face with the sleeve of my hoodie and continue running toward home.

I have to get away from here.

I have to get away from here.

I have to get the hell away from here.

27

**My mom is standing on the front steps as I run toward
our house. She is laying in wait for me I can tell.** No doubt
Ms. Plunkett has been on the phone to her. I slow down my pace
as I approach the stairs.

"Hey Mom! When did you get back from Auntie Laura's?"

*I will be sweet as pie. I will not be what they all expect, prickly
and miserable. I will not arouse suspicion.*

"Addie, darling, are you feeling all right? Joyce in the office
said you were the color of blue cheese when you left the building
sweetheart. How can I help?"

Hmm. I miscalculated. Joyce, from the front office. This is good.

"Cafeteria food, Mom. I forgot my lunch this morning." I say
as my stomach lurches once more and I stumble up the stairs
toward the bathroom.

"Oh Addie I hope it's not…."

I am distracted by the volcanic action of my stomach and am deaf to conversation.

"Mom, Sorry but I can't stop to chat." I extend my left arm out to the side of me to keep her from detaining me.

"Right." Mom grimaces as she gets out of my way. I'll get you some ginger ale and put it in your room. It will settle your tummy. You don't look so good, Addie. You better get some rest." I hear all this as the screen door slams behind me.

Finally I am home. Safe. Quiet. A sanctuary with a bathroom and a bedroom complete with a waning moon.

I pull off my hoodie, t-shirt and jeans. I slide into my green and blue flannel plaid jammies that my mom has laid out on my bed. I peek out of my curtains. The moon should make an appearance soon. I crawl from the end of my bed to my lump of pillows. My head hurts. My stomach is in a knot and the can of ginger ale on my nightstand is just what I need. My mom has put a pink bendy straw in the can. Cute.

From this corner of my room I can see the shift in the angle of light from the sun through my window. The afternoon is coming to a close, fall is sleepy and is tired of bright summer light. There is a sadness inside and outside. Endings are never easy.

The incoming indigo blue of twilight brings with it my moon. I am nervous. Last time we spoke I wasn't very friendly. I hope it has forgiven me.

"You are looking a little thinner than you did last week at this time." I say to my less than full friend.

"Last week you were so grapefruit round." My conversation is awkward and stilted. "Oh hey! It's Halloween this week remember? I hope you will come out and watch all the little kids come through the "Spooktacular Garage" that my mom has made."

The moon is looking at me, staring actually, as if I am a madwoman. It is keeping a steady watch but it is pretending it can't hear me, it is acting as if it doesn't even know me and it is looking right through me.

I am totally alone in my room with only myself to blame.

The week drags on. The sun still shines but not for me. The moon still rises. But it is not the same. There is no more sea of tranquility. Just dis – ease. The school sent home some homework after my mom called and said that I wasn't going to be in for the rest of the week. I was too ill. I will get to it, eventually. After the weekend maybe. After I win ten straight games of solitaire. After.

It is finally Saturday. The longest freakin' week of my life. This is the first time in six days that I have spent more than ten minutes out of my room. I need a perspective that does not involve my ceiling. I need to see an angle of light that isn't from a streetlamp. I have spent the week moping and locked in a vortex of self-loathing. It has not been fun and I look like hell. However, the look is good for the circumstances. Tonight I need to look as ghoulish as I can – Mom and Dad and I are manning the garage and handing out candy to the local urchins. This is the event that I have been waiting for all week.

I stand up to put my Peter Rabbit mug in the dishwasher and clean up my morning mess. Across the cul de sac I see, framed by my kitchen window, Bernerd. He is looking extraordinarily thin. I imagine dark shadows under his eyes. There is a grey cast to his skin and he is trying to shut off his car alarm. He looks so Dracula. He must be throwing himself into the part. The hearse horn has been honking on and off for about the last ten minutes. I watch as Bernerd paces from under the hood of the car to the front seat. I see the keys in his left hand as he gets out from behind the steering wheel and slams with a flourish the hearse door. He moves back under the hood and I can see a rather angry arm movement and then silence. I watch as Bernerd slams the hood of the hearse with a handful of wire. I hear him swear through the window. He must be angry. He is very loud. Bernerd never swears. I wonder what is going on over there. I wonder how Sigge is doing. I'll wonder like crazy, but I won't do anything about it. They don't need me. The Baxters don't need any more Addie induced trouble.

The Bernerd show is over so I will continue with my day. I can hear my mom putting the final touches on the decorations in the garage. I think I will pop my head in and say 'hello, I am alive, do you need any help?'

As I approach the inside hall door to the garage I hear a faint clink of glass, like bottles being placed in a box or something. It is a familiar sound that scares me. My mom has been left to her own devices this past week. I have been home, hiding, and she has been...I have no idea what she has been doing. I fling open the door and whack my toe in the process.

"Owwww." I howl.

"Addie, Addie. For heaven's sake. What is it? Are you all right?" My mom is all wide-eyed and breathless.

"Just my toe. I whacked it with the door. Nothing serious." I look to see if she looks guilty or suspicious. "Whatchya doin'?"

"Juss cleaning up a little. I am happy to see you are up and about. I was beginning to wonder if you were ever going to leave your room. You should really open a window in there. It muss be a little ripe by now…"

Is it my imagination or is she slurring her words?

"Are you okay, Mom? Do you need me out here, at all, for any little thing? I am happy to help."

"No my little copper penny I am juss, fine. I am perfect. I haven't felt this good in weeks. Really. Really. Really. Fannnnnnnnnnntassssssssstic."

Mom's very relaxed.

"Okay. So what are you going to wear as a costume tonight, may I ask?"

"Well Addie, I found the cutest witch costume. It has a poofy skirt with shiny plastic candy corn all over it. I have some green and black striped socks that will look very witchy underneath with my boots, and the best part is I have manufactured a giant wart for my nose, that is complete with a black wiry hair. Put all of these components together with a bit of green grease paint and I am a Dotty Witch!. Hah! Did you get that Addie? I am a dotty witch!"

This last statement sends my mom into a cackling frenzy followed by consumptive coughing.

"Okay, Mom, okay. Hilarious. What is dad going to wear?"

"Honestly Addie your father's costume is juss inshpired. He decided to go as the Mummy! He is wrapping himself in rags and duct tape. Simply hysterical stuff dear. You will love our costumes. What are you going to wear?" Mom is very animated and exhuberant.

"I am, as yet, still undecided, Mom. I have a couple more hours to transform myself. I will think of something though. Don't worry."

"I am not the least bit concerned, Addie. You never let us down." Mom sidles over to me and flings her arm around my shoulders and says in a very conspiratorial tone, "Not like that Lindsay Dixon, girl. What a disappointment she turned out to be."

"Mom! Bob and Dot are friends of yours and Dad's. I know there have been problems but when Dad and I went out with them last weekend,it was obvious that they really need your friendship. I am rather surprised that you would say that Mom! Really. I am going to get ready. Dad will be home from work in a bit so I suggest if you want the bathroom you should get ready too. Oh and thanks for reminding me. I was supposed to do something for Lindsay last week and I forgot. I better get on it. If you need help, call me. The garage is amazing by the way. I can hardly wait to see it with the lights and the sound effects."

"I know, right? It ish quite fannnnnnntassssssssstic and spooky ishn't it."

The unfortunate part of this whole situation is that the garage is not the scariest thing in the neighbourhood.

But these feelings are only suspicions about my mother, not facts. I must send Lindsay the photo evidence from my camera, like I said I would. The fact is that she and Lola really were at St. Andrews and are not the wild vandals the rumour mill has made them out to be.

Little kids start trick or treating really early. It is dusk at five and the first little goblins will be at the door by five-o-two. We let the really little ones go through the garage with all of the lights on and without sound effects. There is no point in scarring the psyches of the littlest of devils before they reach adolescence. Parents and their kids walk through ooohing and ahhhing at my mother's handiwork. She really is a talented artist and craftsperson. The strips of black plastic and the sparkly pink and green skeletons are more fun than scary when it is not dark.

When the little kids are all at home and in their sugar frenzies that is when my mom and dad will make their appearances. In years past Dad has been Frankenstein who emerges from a coffin, when you least expect it, and I have been various and sundry trolls and goblins that scuttle between peoples legs and tickle them on the back of the neck with feathers when they are distracted by the spectacle of dad. Mom was Morticia from the Addams Family once and looked really good being her. She wore an ankle length black wig and a form fitting black sequined dress that had roots for a hemline. *Hmm I wonder if she still has that dress.*

Tonight though, there is a sinister edge to my mom's costume. Her lipstick is somewhat askew and much larger than the actual outline of her lips. She is extraordinarily green and her cackle is maniacal. At the entrance of the garage, she stands stirring a giant cauldron with a broom handle. Dry ice creates a thick misty condensation that wafts steam-like into the air. Mom has placed a green up-light beside the cauldron that accentuates whatever lines and shadows she has created on her face. She looks like one of the hags from Macbeth. She is drinking from a crystal skull-shaped beer mug that she brought home from one of her trips to Vegas. I don't know what she is swilling but she is talking like a sailor and has a red juice moustache. She is very much a traditional Halloween witch.

Dad looks completely amazing. The rags and duct tape combination work really well to create his Mummy persona. Mom has created intense charcoal eyes on Cliffie that look really haunted and bruised peeking out through the bandages. His knees are taped really tightly so he walks in a very strange stiff legged way. Likewise his elbows are taped so he cannot bend them. When he moves his arms they move from the shoulder and that is all. Very authentic Mummy by my Mummy! Hah.

It is totally dark by 6:30 and there is a line-up of kids waiting to get into the garage. I knew this would happen. My mom should have more confidence in her skills. She is an awesome designer. The sound effects range from shrill screaming to the Bach Fugue and heart beats. I had to suggest that to my dad so that I would have some vestige of Dracula in my life.

Cliffie made the music to correspond with the lights. However, it's not as complicated or as impressive as it sounds. I sit at the back of the garage and flick the lights on and off in time to the music. We are so technologically challenged it hurts. My mom and dad are the stars of the show this year. Mom has created an extravaganza for the neighbourhood that they will never forget. Unfortunately my Pippi Longstocking costume is really lame. I am glad to be in the back in the corner in the dark flipping the switch and watching the kids scream and carry on as my dad sneaks up on them and drags lengths of fabric over their faces while he growls and makes scary eye movements.

My mom is really in character. She is spinning the broom stick and stirring the cauldron as if it is all real. She is cackling and talking to herself. She giggles and says things like "bat wings are delicious things" and a toe a day keeps the podiatrist away…". She keeps dipping the mug into the pot and drinking the contents in giant gulps. At the beginning of the night she was pretending to fill her mug but from my perch in the corner I can see that now that there are no toddlers and babies to scare, mom is heavy into the creation that she has made in her cauldron.

Dad can hardly move and seeing what is going on with mom is difficult. The bandages cover his eyes in a criss-cross diagonal way and he can only see a couple of inches in front of him. He is so busy scaring people that I doubt that he has even noticed a change in mom's behaviour. He probably figures it is all part of the act.

I am going to try and get a sample of her cauldron and see what she is drinking.

"Dad, er, Mummy! Listen. It's your favourite song "The Monster Mash". Grab mom and dance. It will be hysterical."

Dad takes the bait. He grabs mom by the hand and dances her into the middle of the driveway, away from the garage and away from the cauldron. I couldn't have planned it better myself. I sneak up to the mug that mom has left sitting on the floor, pick it up and take a slurp. It figures. Crantini. Light on the cran , heavy on the 'tini'. This is so not good.

The song ends and my dad deposits Dee back on her broomstick. She looks dizzy from the twirling. At the end of the driveway I can see Lindsay and her parents. They are obviously debating whether to risk coming through the scary garage or just wave from the cul de sac. I hear Lindsay yell,

"Tell Addie thanks, Mr. Sinclair. She really helped me out!"

"Tell her yourself Linds. She's back here manning the lights!"

Lindsay starts the trek up the driveway and back into my corner of the garage. Before she gets to me my witchy mom, grabs Lindsay's sleeve, and pulls her face to face with her.

"You are no different you know. You are just the same, just the freakin' same. You are not all that you think you are. You are you. You are a punk kid just like the others. Punk, Punk, punk…"

"Okay Mom that is more witchiness and method acting than Lindsay needs."

Lindsay looks at me and shakes her head.

"I can't believe that the cemetery freaked you out so badly last week, Addie. Your mom is a serious freak-show!"

"Was that good Lindsay? Did I scare the living daylights out of you?" Mom realizes what she has done. She knows she needs to continue my lie.

"That was really good Mrs. Sinclair." Lindsay shares.

" I know it was a very long time ago but I was a thessssssss-pian." Mom offers.

Lindsay rolls her eyes at me.

"I know, right? Who knew she could act?" I roll my eyes right back at her. " Parents are such a challenge."

My mom smiles a gentle unscary undemonic smile, and Lindsay accepts it as part and parcel of the act.

"You are very good Mrs. Sinclair, really. You must be where Addie gets her talent from."

"Why thank-you again Lindsay. Some day you should come over and I will show you photos of my university performance days. Stellar times they were." Mom backs away from Lindsay and executes a perfect Elizabethan curtsey.

Good grief. I give my mom the hairy eyeball and she scuttles back to the safety of her cauldron. She knows she is busted.

"BTW Addie. Thanks for the photos. The hot water I was in is now only luke warm. Thanks for that. When are you coming back to school?" asks Lindsay.

"Well I thought it might be next week, but as of right now, who knows. I will keep you posted. Thanks for the thanks. See ya."

160

I watch Lindsay walk back to her parents at the end of our driveway. I am not prepared for what I see. Mr. and Mrs. Dixon and my dad are talking to Mrs. And Mr. Baxter? What the what?

My mom is stirring and staring into her cauldron. She is not participating in the neighbourly confab. I am standing dumbfounded watching as Sigge watches from her driveway, equally silent and confused.

The moon presides over all of us, yanks our blood, pulls our tides, and binds us together in the dark.

29

Judging from the number of thank-you phone calls we have received from our neighbours this morning, Mom's garage was a hit with the kids and their parents. I lost count of the number of bags of candy that we went through but I know for a fact that the cauldron consumed two bottles of vodka and one bottle of cranberry juice, a dozen limes, and one can of club soda. Apparently my mom and the kids had fun.

My dad was disappointed that Dee had not informed him or invited him to the party in the garage. He was surprised when she told him she would like to go in to see her Dr. tomorrow morning and make the necessary arrangements for getting into a rehab program. She sat both dad and I down around the kitchen table and told us that she can't do this on her own. She needs more help to kick her alcohol and drug dependency. She has enjoyed her three weeks doing the things she loves to do and she thought she could do it all alone but nu-uh. The scary stuff that went on here last weekend that she read about in the paper and the sadness that she has seen this past week has made it very difficult for her to carry on without help. She knows what she needs, and she feels she is on the road to becoming an "Eric". She is afraid and we are not able to help her anymore.

Whoa. I am slapped stupid by her "Eric" connection.

There are no tears. What can you say when you know that someone you love is making a good decision? You say "You are making a good decision. Congratulations." So that is what dad and I said. Tomorrow there may be tears but today, not even one. We will all take down the Halloween decorations carefully and deliberately, put them into boxes and hope that next year will be an even better event. We will put this year away into a box in the basement. We will open it in the future and hope we will see it as shiny and untarnished.

Just before I closed the garage door last night I watched as the Baxters and the Dixons walked together to their respective homes. I could hear them laughing as they talked about my dad's mummy dance and the wonderfully scary and believeable characterization of my mother. They were all so complimentary, so forgiving, so adult, even if they suspected the truth. I watched Sigge's solitary figure looking toward my house, anticipating her parents, and ultimately, a wave of a hand, a gesture from me, proving that I had not forgotten her.

I waved, and she waved and I imagined a small white flag had emerged from the tip of my fingers. I surrendered under a sliver of a moon and now I must confess.

But not right this second.

This is my Monday Morning Mental Memo.

1. Call Dr. Gilbert. Take my mom into see him.

2. Call Ms. Plunkett. Take myself into see her.

3. Call my dad a velour-wearing mummy.

4. Pack my mom's suitcase.

5. Call the Baxters and say welcome home to Mr. B.

6. Sit under the bleachers in the dark and listen to a Dracula rehearsal.

7. Repeat # 3 and #6 daily.

Ms. Plunkett was able to see me first thing this morning. Lucky me. I find myself outside her office door by eight fifteen. I really need to see her and I really need to get a few things off of my chest. Her office door is open, there is a steaming cup of green tea on her desk, and the scent of lavender in the air. I will wait for her before I go in. I don't want to be accused of anything new and excitingly deadly.

I can hear her approaching as the sound of tinkling bells and jangling bangle bracelets is a dead giveaway. She rounds the corner and is resplendent in a tie-died black and white skirt, a black and white hounds tooth jacket, a purple turtleneck, red socks and sandals. Her hair is wild and free and she is smiling.

"Good morning Addie! What a marvellous Monday. Did you enjoy Halloween as much as I did? I just love to see all the little kids come to the door don't you? They are all so excited for candy and their costumes that they just vibrate as they stand on the doorstep. It's darling. It has been such a long time since my kids were little I really enjoy the day. Now it's all naughty nurses and pouty policewomen. Hardly cute! Yikes."

"It's my favourite day of the year, actually." I say, looking at my feet. It is hard to meet her level of energy so early in the day.

"So, what brings you in here so early? Are you feeling better? You certainly look much less green than the last time we met. Sometimes taking some time to think and digest the events that occur in our worlds is very healing. Was it a quiet and thought provoking week?" Ms. Plunkett looks at me with intense all-seeing eyes that are hard not to stare into.

"Actually, it was the hardest week of my life. I did a horrible thing, Ms. Plunkett. I abandoned my best friends and I lied to them and I haven't been able to talk to them and I am so freakin' embarrassed and scared to reveal what I did. It has been eating me up! Last week should have been amazing and fun and the best year of my life so far, but it was the nastiest, second worst, nah, the very worst week of my life. And today Ms. Plunkett it has got to end. I can't live with this any longer. My mom is going to try to get into rehab today. That is where I am going after this, and before she goes and I get wrapped up in all that emotion I need to dump my emotional baggage and I am sorry but it has to be on you. You seem to like it when I do so here I am."

"Addie, I really enjoy listening to you talk. You have an energy that is well, quite different from most people and the way you tell a story is very entertaining. I am glad that you feel that you can talk to me. I am flattered."

" Okay then Ms. P.. Settle in now. You might change your opinion of me when I tell you what I did, but hey. That is the chance that I have to take. Here goes. I am the person responsible for revealing the Baxter's address to Eric. I am the reason why Mr. Baxter was hurt. I am the reason why my neighbourhood was terrorized. I am the reason, Ms. Plunkett. Now do you see why I couldn't come to school. Why I couldn't and shouldn't communicate with the Baxters? I am responsible. I am bad news Addie. It seems that whenever I get involved with someone's life, poof, bad news, bad stuff happens. I am a vortex of doom Ms. Plunkett. DOOM!"

A smile creeps across Ms. Plunkett's face. She has been listening to me really intently, but when I say that I am the vortex of doom, her teeth make an appearance. She starts to giggle.

"Adelaide. Wow. You have been carrying a lot of grief and guilt around with you but the vortex of doom dear? I don't think so. You are just a girl who has been involved with some unfortunate circumstances. You are not responsible. You did not hit Mr. Baxter. You did not pour alcohol down your mother's throat. You did not break into your own house and tape your father to a chair. You did none of these things Addie. How are you responsible?"

"I am responsible because I didn't tell anyone about my meeting with Kevin. I am responsible because I showed him where the Baxter's live! That is why I am responsible. If I had not answered Sigge's phone, if I had not met with him, if , if, if, …SEEEEE! I am responsible for all of this. And I am so sorry Ms. Plunkett. My stomach is in a giant knot, I bailed on Dracula and let Mr. Noble down, my head hurts, my mom is a mess, and it's all my fault."

``Addie. Who is Kevin?"

"Kevin is Eric. I just found that out last week. Eric was pretending to be Kevin, the Baxter's cousin, and that his mom was planning a 50th birthday party for Mr. B. and he had no idea where they lived since they moved and…"

"Had you ever met Eric Baxter, Addie?"

"Nope and I hadn't even seen a picture of him, until I saw a picture of who I thought was Kevin sitting on the counter in the Baxter's kitchen last weekend. All I know is the Baxter's have a third kid that I know virtually nothing about. See? It was me."

"What I hear Addie is that you were duped. You were tricked into doing something you wouldn't normally do. Honestly Addie, if "Kevin" had said that he was a drug addict and that he needed to know where the Baxter's lived so that he could break in and steal stuff, would you have revealed anything at all?"

"I am not that stupid."

" I know you are not, Addie, and that is exactly my point. If you knew the truth about Eric it wouldn't have happened. You are not responsible for hurting anyone. You thought you were doing a nice thing for someone. Eric did all the wrong things, Addie. You did not."

"Oh man. Ms. Plunkett. But still, if…"

"If is a tiny word with huge impact, Addie. Don't worry about the ifs. What happened happened. Let' s just move forward from here. You are a good person Addie. Don't forget that. You were trying to be helpful. That's what you need to remember."

"Thanks Ms. Plunkett, but I still feel weird and sick."

" I am sure you will fix that in time, Addie. I am glad you came in today. Will I see you at group tonight?"

"Maybe. It might be just what I need. See you later. I am going to sign out now," I say, "and just so you know, Ms. P., Mondays don't feel so marvellous."

30

Dracula rehearsals begin at 3:15. It is 2:45, the drama room is deserted so I can scoot under the bleachers undetected. I have to know how things are progressing, how Lola is as Lucy, if Bernerd is a scary as he looks these days.

I have brought along a copy of the script that I bought at Aqua Books. I have read and re-read Lucy's dialogue until it has become my own. I know this character better than I know me. That makes sense I guess. I am way more dimensional than ink on paper.

I hear a rustling at the far end of the bleachers. Papers fall down through the seats. Someone jumps down and starts to rummage around trying to locate their papers. That someone is Bernerd. Good thing I am dressed in black today. I blend. I can hear his breathing. It is magnified wonderfully by the silence of the room and the confines of the bleachers.

Wonderfully? Whoa.

I am only saved from detection by the sound of the drama room door opening and Mr. Noble's shoes clicking across the floor.

"Bernerd? Why are you under the bleachers? I thought you were a rodent. Let's get started please. Lola will not be joining us today. She seems to be conspicuous in her absence. Take your place on stage. Now. Notice how we have the piece of glass suspended from the ceiling and on an angle? Well that is going to be the window once the set is built but it is also going to be one of our best theatrical tricks in the show. We will have a giant stuffed bat mounted behind the glass, there will be smoke, it will look like a transformation takes place. It will be magic. Which reminds me, we will actually have a magician help us pull off some of these tricks. This is a melodrama Bernerd and we are going to milk it for all it is worth!"

"Yessir." Bernerd turns up one corner of his mouth into a kind of smirk.

I recognize that look. But I don't recognize a lot of Bernerd at this second. He is exceptionally thin. He has a scruffy beard and is awfully pale. He looks unwell, perhaps, undead. Maybe he is trying to look like this. I hope he is. I hope it is nothing more. I hope it is not my fault he looks like this.

"Okay Bernerd," begins Mr. Noble. "Take it from line 36. You are talking to Lucy. She feels she has disappointed you and that you are angry with her. Forgive her Bernerd, with your eyes and with your words. Believe what you are saying and deliver it as if you mean it and that Lucy is really here. When you are ready..."

Mr. Noble backs away from the front of the stage, he turns off all of the lights in the drama room except for a follow spot.

Bernerd is standing in a puddle of moon on the stage. He is in the middle of a perfect circle, center stage, staring straight out into the audience. He collects himself, clears his throat, and as if he knows I am here he says,

"Oh! LUCY. I cannot be angry with YOU. Nor can I be angry with MY FRIEND whose happiness is YOURS…"

"Um Bernerd?"Mr Noble looks confused. "Why are you putting such strange emPHAsis on your dialogue? Could we try it again proPERly this time?"

"Of course, sir. I was trying to make a point. I will begin again.'

"Oh Lucy. I cannot be angry with you. Nor can I be angry with my friend whose happiness is yours…"

"Was that better?" Bernerd asks.

"Much, much better." The words escape my mouth before I know it is happening.

Ohmigawd.

"I concur, mysterious drama room voice. Did you hear that Bernerd or am I hallucinating?" Mr. Noble asks.

" Hear what sir?" Bernerd smiles. "I didn't hear a thing."

"I have had an excrutiatingly long day, Bernerd. "I seem to be hearing things. Let's call it quits for this afternoon, shall we. We will make up for it tomorrow. Have a good evening."

Mr. Noble and Bernerd switch off the light and the room is totally dark. I will wait six minutes and then I will leave. It is one thing to be caught but it is totally another to be found.

Group begins precisely at seven o'clock. I arrive early to get a seat next to Ms. Plunkett. She is safe and warm and she sits at the top of the circle. I am going to speak first tonight. To get this all over with. It's time.

Perry Adler toddles in. He is still wearing his striped pants and a dog collar but on him it is cute. He would loathe the word cute to be used to describe him but it's true. Cute is the nastiest thing I will ever say about him because he kicks really hard. Truth. Anyway, Dakota is here, there are a few new faces but we will all be aware of one another by the end of the evening. Dr. Rubin clicks his loafers over to a chair next to me and I wait for Ms. Plunkett to arrive. I am excited for tonight.

Finally. Ms. Plunkett opens one of the annex doors and secures it. She opens the other door and secures it. Her hair is big but she doesn't need this big of a space. There is banging about in the hallway and then a reason for the two door entrance. Sigge is dragging a huge canvas into the annex. It looks like the one my mom gave her a couple of weeks ago. The face of the canvas is covered so none of us can see it. I can hardly wait for the reveal. Ms. P and Sigge lean the painting up against a wall, and Sigge takes a seat right beside me. Ms. Plunkett finds another chair across the room.

Wow.

I didn't expect this. Sigge, next to me.

"So everyone, hello again. As you probably noticed Sigge brought a visual aid this evening!"

Ms. Plunkett knows how to work a room. We all laugh quietly.

We are all polite and well behaved, right this second at least.

Dr. Rubin starts things off.

"We have had some turmoil in our neighbourhood in the past couple of weeks. It has been disruptive and hurtful to many of our families. I hope you all treat one another with respect and kindness. This has not been an easy time for any and all involved. Play nice, please. Now that that elephant has been dealt with… Who would like to speak this evening?"

Sigge jumps up before I have a chance to shoot my hand in the air. Damn, she's quick. She too looks tired and full of shadows. But underneath the cloudiness I sense some bubbles of fun trying to emerge. Sigge looks down at me and smiles a tentative wiggly grin. It's a safe smile. I accept it as a quiet gift and sorta smile back. It has been a really long, lonely week.

"Okay everyone. Here's the thing. It was my brother, Eric Baxter, that was responsible for the turmoil that Dr. Rubin speaks of. Eric is a meth addict. Eric assaulted my dad and left him for dead. This has been the crappiest week of my life. I was abandoned but recently reclaimed by my best friend, and my brother Bernerd is really Dracula as a result of this horror that we are living through. Eric broke into every house, or tried to, on our cul de sac. He rattled everyone's nerves. He however, has been arrested, and is in custody. He used to be a really nice guy, but now he's a meth. Hah!"

Every jaw on every person in the room drops when Sigge says this. We are all thinking that this is no time to laugh, that she is strong and amazing and boy kinda, well, hard.

"Sorry. Sometimes you just have to laugh. If it wasn't for that bad joke that Addie's dad made up on the spot for my brother Bernerd I don't know what he and I would have done. Every time we look at one another we say things like 'What a fine meth you have gotten us into this time and "What a meth you made". I know it sounds crazy, but it helps. Thank your dad for me please would you Addie?" Sigge looks directly at me. Honest, open and very sincere.

"Sure Sigge." I look at the floor and stifle a smirk. My dad is a complete, fabulous, nut.

I am so proud of my dad I could burst. Who knew the velour king could be so solid, and funny and cool? But my mom, well, not so much. I am glad she's seeking help, but I am pissed that it had to happen right now. Doesn't she know drama is for the young and the restless and the stage? That she and Eric and guilt the size of Antarctica are the reasons I am here right now and not lollygagging upside down in my room talking to the moon about a boy I like that has steely...

"So Sigge. Let's see your picture." Dakota, one of the regulars, requests. " It's huge."

I am jarred off of my cloud by Dakota's request. Once I get a chance to speak I will mom-vent and try to understand how she went off the rails, again, this time. How I was too preoccupied to notice, how none of this, this recovery, is easy for me. Or any of us here, for that matter.

Sigge takes the sheet off of her canvas with a giant flourish, as if she is the Darkside Avenger and wearing a cape, and I am not surprised. The canvas is covered in blue plastic rose petals, and three silver sparkle ghost-like images of Bernerd and Sigge and me. We are all walking hand in hand toward a vortex of bright white light. It's almost beautiful in its sadness and optimism and sparkle glitter, but it is so freakin' cheesy and actually really embarrassing. But hey, what do I expect, that's Sigge. It's her painting and she can be as lame as she wants. A happy ending, like on the canvas, is way too easy though. If I could paint it would be some swirling black tornado that sucks the life out of all who see it. No incredible lightness of being. (Thanks Ms. O.) The only happy thing about tonight is that Bernerd and Sigge's dad is okay. The stuff surrounding why we are happy is anything but positive. Eric is in jail. Eric has caused his family loads of anguish that they now have to work through. None of this will be easy. But tonight I will pretend that everything will be okay because of the painting. That Sigge has fixed our world with art. That I am fine, transformed and transcendent, and that I can levitate or some fool thing. I will do whatever it takes to make her as happy as she can be, whatever will make me look less guilt-ridden. Whatever.

A collective wave of appreciation for Sigge's painting rolls around the circle. Words like striking and really pretty and amazing are smiled in Sigge's direction. I congratulate her too. When we are finally ready to move onto other topics, I really can no longer wait. I shoot up my hand and wave it around like a wild thing. I am so desperate to speak,

"Hello everyone! My name is Addie Sinclair. And just for the record, I am the Vortex of Doominess!"

Before I can explain, the circle collapses into laughter. I start to laugh too but I stop as Lindsay Dixon skulks into the room.

"Wait. Am I in the right group?" she says, " I thought this would be a weep-fest…."